Liz gulped, e‌‌‌‌‌‌‌‌‌‌nto white-hot ale

"Wh-what are you‌‌‌‌‌‌‌‌‌‌nd she was suddenly‌‌‌‌‌‌‌‌‌‌ her breath.

He danced her slowly backward, toward the wall. "Putting your willpower and integrity to the test."

The feel of his hands moving up her arms, to her shoulders, then her neck, then her face, sent a shimmer of need sifting through her. "Travis…."

He ran his thumbs along her jaw, then her lips, the soft encouraging pressure parting them. "I'm not your client any more, Liz." He touched his mouth to hers. Briefly. Testingly.

"I'm not even your friend."

He bent his head and kissed her again, his lips tenderly coaxing and recklessly taking, the sensuality of his mouth moving over hers, until she wreathed her arms about his neck and kissed him back, every bit as passionately and deeply as he was kissing her.

Dear Reader,

When I created the fictional town of Laramie, Texas, I wanted it to embody all the best qualities of the Lone Star State. Hence, it had to be a place where people dreamed big and knew through hard work and determination that anything was possible. It had to be a place where love was boundless. Family mattered. Neighbors helped each other out. Generosity of spirit and honorable behavior was the norm.

Readers responded by falling in love with the setting as surely as I had, and now, the fictional town of Laramie, Texas, is home to twenty-four novels. (All now available as ebooks.) The McCabes of Texas miniseries—the stories about John and Lilah McCabe's four bold, handsome sons—started the McCabe family dynasty. The answers to those four men were the four orphaned sisters in The Lockharts of Texas. Sam McCabe, his five rowdy sons and feisty Kate Marten were the subject of *Texas Vows*, a single-title novel. The McCabes: Next Generation focused on the six offspring of Sam and Kate Marten McCabe. Texas Legacies: The Carrigans featured the four offspring of Meg Lockhart and Luke Carrigan. And Texas Legacies: The McCabes recounts the love stories of the offspring of Greta and Shane McCabe.

Now, I introduce to you my new series, The Legends of Laramie County, with four memorable new Texas clans. We start with the Cartwrights—four generations of Texas lady ranchers who suddenly find themselves in need of a…man?

For more information on these and other books please visit me on the web at www.cathygillenthacker.com.

Happy reading!

Cathy Gillen Thacker

The Reluctant Texas Rancher

Cathy Gillen Thacker

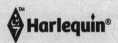

TORONTO NEW YORK LONDON
AMSTERDAM PARIS SYDNEY HAMBURG
STOCKHOLM ATHENS TOKYO MILAN MADRID
PRAGUE WARSAW BUDAPEST AUCKLAND

If you purchased this book without a cover you should be aware that this book is stolen property. It was reported as "unsold and destroyed" to the publisher, and neither the author nor the publisher has received any payment for this "stripped book."

Recycling programs
for this product may
not exist in your area.

ISBN-13: 978-0-373-75398-7

THE RELUCTANT TEXAS RANCHER

Copyright © 2012 by Cathy Gillen Thacker

All rights reserved. Except for use in any review, the reproduction or utilization of this work in whole or in part in any form by any electronic, mechanical or other means, now known or hereafter invented, including xerography, photocopying and recording, or in any information storage or retrieval system, is forbidden without the written permission of the publisher, Harlequin Enterprises Limited, 225 Duncan Mill Road, Don Mills, Ontario M3B 3K9, Canada.

This is a work of fiction. Names, characters, places and incidents are either the product of the author's imagination or are used fictitiously, and any resemblance to actual persons, living or dead, business establishments, events or locales is entirely coincidental.

This edition published by arrangement with Harlequin Books S.A.

For questions and comments about the quality of this book please contact us at Customer_eCare@Harlequin.ca

® and TM are trademarks of the publisher. Trademarks indicated with ® are registered in the United States Patent and Trademark Office, the Canadian Trade Marks Office and in other countries.

www.Harlequin.com

Printed in U.S.A.

ABOUT THE AUTHOR

Cathy Gillen Thacker is married and a mother of three. She and her husband spent eighteen years in Texas and now reside in North Carolina. Her mysteries, romantic comedies and heartwarming family stories have made numerous appearances on bestseller lists, but her best reward, she says, is knowing one of her books made someone's day a little brighter. A popular Harlequin Books author for many years, she loves telling passionate stories with happy endings, and thinks nothing beats a good romance and a hot cup of tea! You can visit Cathy's website at www.cathygillenthacker.com for more information on her upcoming and previously published books, recipes and a list of her favorite things.

Books by Cathy Gillen Thacker

HARLEQUIN AMERICAN ROMANCE

*The McCabes: Next Generation
**Texas Legacies: The Carrigans
†Made in Texas
‡The Lone Star Dads Club
†Texas Legacies: The McCabes

Chapter One

"We have to face facts. We need a man and we need one bad," eighty-three-year-old Tillie Cartwright said, the moment the four women sat down on the porch of the ranch house.

"Like heck we do." Sixty-six-year-old Faye Elizabeth handed out the corn to be shucked. "Men are nothing but trouble. Always have been. Always will be."

"But they have their uses." Forty-eight-year-old Reba winked. "And with my sciatica acting up again…" She winced as she tried to get her aching hip and thigh settled comfortably in the cushioned wicker chair. "I don't know any other way to manage. Unless…"

All eyes turned to the youngest member of the family.

Liz Cartwright shook her head at the three generations of Cartwright women in front of her. Under any other circumstance this conversation would have been ludicrous, but on the estrogen-powered Four Winds cattle ranch, where she had grown up and now resided once again, the ornery, fiercely opinionated comments were to be expected.

"I'm not giving up my law practice to run this ranch," Liz said with the full conviction of her twenty-eight years. It didn't matter how much pressure her mother tried to exert. "I said I would help out—and I will—but other than that, the most I'm prepared to do is help you choose a new ranch hand."

"Then it's a good thing I'm here," a deep male voice interjected.

An audible gasp filled the air as Travis Anderson walked around the side of the house and climbed onto the porch. The tall, oh-so-sexy cowboy removed his hat, revealing thick dark hair in need of a cut, and charcoal-gray eyes.

His respects paid, Travis settled the Stetson squarely on his head and smiled. "Isn't that right, ladies?"

TRAVIS HAD FIGURED Liz Cartwright would not be all that excited to see him. The two of them had dated in high school. She still resented him for the way he had ended it.

"We're looking for a ranch hand, Travis," Liz told him drily as she ripped a chunk of green husk and silk from a cob. "Not a Houston attorney."

Travis knew the Laramie County rumor mill had been working overtime since he had arrived home a few days ago, suitcase in hand.

Liz was apparently curious, too. Though he doubted his savvy fellow attorney would come right out and admit it.

After taking in the way the spring sunlight brought out the fire in her shoulder-length, auburn hair, he studied the skeptical twist to her pink lips.

It didn't matter that Liz was more beautiful than ever, or that her fair skin looked just as soft to the touch. And the fact she was sexy in an unconscious, girl-he'd-grown-up-with way was of no consequence, either.

What he needed was the opportunity to make a deal.

And this temporary job on the Four Winds Ranch would give him that. As well as a place to stay…

Never one to be taken advantage of, Liz waved a dismissive hand before going on to strip the ear of corn bare and drop it into the bowl. She paused to shoot him a disdainful look. "So maybe you should run along back to the city.…"

Travis shoved his hands in the pockets of his jeans and leaned against the porch rail. As always when they were together, the world seemed to narrow to just the two of them. "Didn't you hear?" he taunted, looking into her emerald eyes. "My days as a bona fide city slicker are over."

Standing abruptly, Liz placed her hands on her slender, jean-clad hips. "Hearing it and believing it to be true are two different things." She let her gaze drift over him before returning ever so deliberately to his eyes. "And why anyone as accomplished as you would give up a downtown loft and a six-figure salary…"

Put that way, Travis knew, his actions didn't make sense. He concentrated on what would. "The loft measured less than six hundred square feet." Casting a glance at Tillie, Faye Elizabeth and Reba, he flashed the kind of disarming smile he used on witnesses he was about to depose, before explaining wryly, "It wasn't a whole lot of space to give up. As for the job…" He turned back to Liz and lifted a hand. "I decided I'm better suited at the moment for a wide-open range and a herd of cattle. Two things you ladies have in spades."

A place, he added silently, *where I'll have plenty of space and privacy to reflect. Plenty of time to plan my next big move…*

Liz folded her arms beneath her breasts. "Neither the

land nor the cattle are for sale, so if that's your angle, Travis Anderson..."

"I do want my own land. My own herd." As well as something even more important to him: an intact reputation. "But while I'm figuring out how I'm going to get those things, I won't mind taking care of yours."

"I VOTE WE HIRE HIM," Liz's mother said, as soon as Travis Anderson walked off to give them a moment to confer.

Tillie shrugged. "He knows cattle."

Faye Elizabeth frowned. "I don't see that we have much choice, given the fix we're in."

"I'm not so sure we have to act this fast," Liz cautioned, with lawyerly calm. "For starters, I don't trust why he's here." Travis had been achievement-oriented his entire life. "I think he has an ulterior motive."

She just wasn't sure what it was.

Liz's mother sized her up with a mischievous grin. "No matter. I'm sure you'll be able to contain yourself around that handsome man. If that's what you want," she teased.

Liz flushed and pushed the distant memory of Travis's kisses away. Kisses she had been too uptight to really enjoy, because she'd been so afraid of having her heart stomped on by the cutest boy in school.

Ignoring the knot of anxiety in her solar plexus, she shook her head. "I didn't mean me. There have been rumors in the legal community that Travis Anderson lost his boy wonder status."

Reba frowned. "That doesn't sound like the Travis I recall. Or anyone with Lockhart and Anderson blood running through his veins. Most members of both families are incredibly successful."

"I didn't believe it, either," Liz admitted with a shake of her head. "Until he showed up here today, looking for work. Now I'm beginning to think there might be something to it. Just as there's more to his asking for work here, of all places."

"Such as?" Tillie prodded.

Liz turned her glance to Travis. Currently, he was inspecting the broken-down, thirty-year-old tractor parked next to the barn.

She remembered him being tall and broad-shouldered. Athletic enough to make all the school teams he wanted. Smart enough to graduate with a whole passel of scholarships. But she didn't remember him being that muscular, or so good at filling out a pair of jeans.

"What could he be up to?" Faye Elizabeth asked, inspecting the shucked corn for any stray strands of silk.

Travis turned. The bemused expression on his face said he knew they were watching him.

Thank heaven he didn't know what Liz was thinking!

Eyebrows raised, he stared at her a long moment, then glanced away.

Aware that everyone was waiting for her to weigh in, Liz turned back to them, her pulse racing.

She pushed aside the desire welling up inside her. This was no time to be thinking about kissing Travis again.

"I don't know." She sighed. "Despite what he says, I can't see him ever giving up the law to ranch." Liz knew how hard Travis Anderson had worked for everything he'd earned, how deeply wedded he was to all his plans. "It wouldn't matter what kind of professional disappointment he has weathered. He would still pick himself up, dust himself off and keep right on going toward his goal." Whatever the latest one was.

Reba shrugged. "Sounds to me like Travis has finally come to his senses, in wanting to return to the ranching life he was born into." She looked at her daughter. "You'd be lucky if you had an epiphany like that, too."

Liz dropped her head in her hands and groaned. Would they never stop wishing she would give up everything to take over the ranch?

Getting back to business, Reba pushed on. "All those in favor of hiring Travis Anderson to ride, rope and wrangle for us, say aye."

"Aye," the three elder Cartwright women said in unison.

Trying not to think about how uncomfortable it would be for her to have Travis around all the time, Liz threw up her hands. "Fine." She was so busy with her law practice, she wasn't going to be here much, anyway.

Faye Elizabeth gathered up the shucked corn and took it into the kitchen to start dinner. Tillie headed back to the ranch books. Only Reba remained on the porch with Liz.

Her mother pointed to the fence, where Travis stood gazing out at the vast, rolling terrain of the ten-thousand-acre Four Winds. "Go get him, and show him to his quarters."

Liz tore her gaze from his handsome profile. She hadn't expected him to sleep on the property, too! Irritably, she demanded, "Which are going to be where?"

"The homestead, of course."

Her mouth fell open. "Wait a minute." Indignant, she angled a thumb at her chest. "I'm sleeping in the homestead."

"You *were*. Now he will be. Unless…" Reba tossed her a speculative look "…you want Travis bunking in the main house with us?"

Her frustration mounting, Liz leaped to her feet. "Why does he have to be on the ranch at all before eight o'clock or after five?" The last thing she needed was a sexy guy she'd once had a crush on underfoot.…

Reba winced and put a hand against her lower back. "Because it's calving season, we barely have the funds to pay one ranch hand and we need someone around to do the heavy lifting at all hours of the day and night."

Liz couldn't argue the necessity of having someone to relieve her mother of the physical rigors of ranch work. However, she *could* disagree with his working conditions. "I know that, Mom, but he has to have time off," she said reasonably.

Reba stretched to relieve the pain. "He can have time off after all the calves are born."

As always, the Cartwright tunnel vision when it came to ranch matters superseded all else, including the needs of others. "Travis may not agree to this," Liz warned.

Reba sent her a confident glance. "Then it's up to you to convince him."

TRAVIS HEARD BOOT STEPS crossing the rough ground, and turned as Liz approached.

The reluctant look on her pretty face told him all he needed to know. He had a temporary job. Likely over her objections.

"I'm ready to start anytime," he drawled, eyeing her in a way it would have been unwise to do earlier, before he got the job.

Her rich auburn hair was just as thick and silky as

he recalled. It was a little shorter now, falling only to her shoulders. But the classic cut and side-swept bangs suited her as much as the slight flush to her cheeks, the hint of temper in her pine-green eyes, and the determined set of her soft, bow-shaped lips.

His presence obviously flustered her, as it always had, in a way he found irresistible.

What was different was that he felt a little off his game around her, too.

As if his ordinary way of tackling people and problems wouldn't work.

To get to know her, to understand the way she ticked, he would have to dig deeper, get past her resistance—as he hadn't been able to do when they were teens.

And given what they needed to accomplish, the sooner he was able to do that the better.

"Tonight, if you want," he continued.

Liz scowled, looking even less thrilled about that. "They figured as much." She cocked her head sideways and sized him up with a wary glance. "You know they expect you to move out here, for as long as you choose to work for the Four Winds Ranch?"

Nodding, Travis ambled closer.

She might be struggling to handle her family, or contain him, but she was still sweet and sharp, with a way of beckoning him near that went far beyond simple chemistry.

Pushing the attraction away, he said, "The ad posted in the feed store said the position included room and board and being on call 24/7." Which made it perfect for him…and his goals.

Liz huffed, clearly as annoyed by his accommodating attitude as she was by his presence. With only a cursory look at the cattle grazing in the pasture beyond, she wheeled around and took off in the opposite direction. "Don't get too excited," she said, tossing a mocking glance over her shoulder. "You haven't seen your quarters yet."

Travis admired the sway of her slender hips and the purposeful way her long legs ate up the ground. He caught up with her, so they were walking side by side. "Does this mean I'll get the room next to yours?"

Liz shot him a drop-dead look and headed toward the one-room log cabin behind the barns. En route, they passed the main ranch house, an angular, U-shaped domicile made of rough-hewn timber and flat-cut stone, with wide porches on the front and back. "Actually, you're getting my room. Or what was my room, once I clear my stuff out. You'll be bunking in the old homestead."

He was close enough to smell the jasmine scent of her perfume. Not a good thing, given what it did to his libido.

He eased back as they reached a field of knee-high grass, interspersed with Texas wildflowers. "Well, that's exciting."

"Not really." Mirroring his ironic tone, Liz paused to open a gate in the weathered wood fence. "It's very primitive."

He shrugged. "There's something to be said for whittling life down to the very basics."

As he was doing today.

It made you reevaluate. Think about what you wanted versus what you needed. It made it easier to set a goal and develop a plan to go after what you had to have to be happy.

Travis was ready to do that, and more.

Liz latched the gate behind them, then carried on.

"You say that now," she predicted. "You may be singing a different tune later."

She really didn't know him. "Does it have indoor plumbing?"

She slanted him a glance from beneath those thick auburn lashes. "As well as electricity. But no real kitchen. So you'll have to take your meals in the main house with us, unless you want to get by on whatever you can store in the minifridge and whip up on a hot plate or microwave."

He ignored her attempt to discourage him. The way her shirt cupped her breasts was not so easy to disregard.

Folding his arms, he tried to ignore the pressure starting at the front of his jeans. "Thanks for the option, but I'm not much of a cook."

Amusement glimmered in her eyes. "Somehow I suspected that would still be the case."

Okay, that was definitely a dig, but he wasn't going to apologize for the single-minded dedication he had given to his path in life. It had gotten him where he wanted to go, and then some. The fact that some of it had recently derailed was his fault, sure, but being here would fix that.

"Faye Elizabeth, on the other hand, is legendary for her culinary skills," Travis continued, with lazy insistence. That was one bonus for being on the ranch, right there.

Liz rolled her eyes. "And there is nothing my grandmother likes more than an appreciative audience for her efforts."

"She'll have that in me," he promised. These days, he would take his pleasure where he could get it.

Liz paused at the door to the homestead. "My question is why are you really doing this?" She eyed him skeptically. "And don't give me that you-just-want-to-be-a-rancher-and-ride-the-open-range bit again, Travis Anderson. Because I'm just not buying it!"

Chapter Two

For a moment, Liz thought Travis wasn't going to answer her. Then he reached into his pocket for his wallet, took a twenty-dollar bill and handed it to her.

She gazed into his intelligent gray eyes, wishing he wasn't such a fine example of masculine intensity. But he was. With the kind of good looks that only got better with age. The sensuality of his lips perfectly complemented his other bold, handsome features. And the rest of him was just as fine. He was six foot three inches of solid, indomitable male, and he used it to his advantage.

Which made his arrival back in Laramie County all the more perplexing.

Doing her best to control the sudden hitch in her breathing, Liz looked down at the bill in her hand and remarked with humor, "I'm dying to know what this is for."

He took off his hat as he followed her inside. "I want to hire you to represent me."

Was he serious? The brooding look in his eyes said he was.

Liz watched him run a hand through dark, tousled hair, which was several weeks past time for a cut. "Well, then it's going to cost you a heck of a lot more than twenty dollars," she said, setting her lingering physical attraction to him aside. "An initial consultation is two hundred dollars." And there were other reasons she should say no, too.

Travis nodded amiably. "Consider that a down payment for helping me clear my name and get my career back on track."

Of all the things he could have confided in her, this was the last Liz ever would have expected. She stared at him in surprise.

"My law license has been suspended for six months. I want you to handle the appeal."

Curiosity won out over common sense. "What did you do?" she asked in shock.

Tensing, Travis looked around the cabin, taking in the brass bed and wooden armoire, the old leather sofa, the table and two chairs. Tucked into the open shelving that served as a pantry was a minifridge, microwave and hot plate. Adjacent to that was an old-fashioned kitchen sink. A small bathroom, with pedestal sink and narrow shower, had been added on.

He turned back to her, clearly not happy about having to admit, "I disappointed a client who is now suing me for legal malpractice."

Silence fell between them. It was impossible to imagine the Travis she had grown up with doing anything unethical or foolish. "Are you still with Haverty, Brockman & Roberts?"

He settled on the arm of the sofa and stretched his legs out. "They asked me to tender my resignation."

Liz edged close enough to be able to see his eyes. In the dim light of the cabin, they were the color of an approaching spring storm.

"So they wouldn't have to pay you severance, right?"

Travis shrugged, the turbulent emotion on his face

fading to acceptance. "I got something out of it, too," he admitted quietly. "It always looks better to resign than to be fired."

True.

The uncomfortable silence between them lengthened.

Travis studied her with narrowed eyes. "What have you heard about what's been going on?" he asked curiously.

"In legal circles? Not much…except whatever you did to vault you off the fast track was being kept very hush-hush by the senior partners."

Travis locked gazes with her. He rested a callused hand on his thigh in a move that wasn't quite as easy and relaxed as it seemed. "Well, that's no longer the case." He exhaled roughly, lips taut. "As of yesterday, the senior partners are letting it be known all over Houston that they are as disappointed in me as my former client is, and they are going to be helping her in the lawsuit being waged against me."

Not good. Not good at all. "In return for keeping Haverty, Brockman & Roberts from being sued, as well?" Liz guessed.

Travis's eyes hardened. "Sacrificing me is the only way they can protect the firm and keep Olympia Herndon's business."

Liz studied him with the same reserve she would have used with any other client. "Why ask me to represent you? Why not go to another big firm—maybe even an HB&R rival—back in Houston?" There were always competitors eager to take another law firm down a notch.

That was the more logical route to go.

But, apparently, not to him.

Travis faced her boldly, his annoyance at having to

explain himself evident. "Everything I have worked for is on the line. I need an attorney I can trust, someone strong and savvy enough to handle this. And you've got a reputation for finding out-of-court solutions where there seem to be none."

That was true. Although, out of courtesy, Liz felt duty-bound to point out, "Your malpractice insurance company can do that for you, Travis."

He grimaced. "They're interested in making the problem go away via a large cash settlement that will not only raise my rates but make it look as if I did something wrong, when I didn't. I want to come out of this with my professional reputation intact."

"So you're asserting that there is no validity to any of the charges against you?"

"Everything I did was in my client's best interest. If the huge business deal Olympia Herndon was chasing had gone through, I have no doubt I would still be representing her. But it didn't. So—" his broad shoulders lifted in a tense shrug "—someone had to take the fall...."

And that someone had been Travis.

"What about your family?" Liz asked quietly, knowing this couldn't be going over well with the Andersons. They would be furious at even the implication that Travis had acted less than admirably.

"They know I quit my job in Houston, although I was vague about the reasons. They don't know about the six-month suspension of my law license, or the lawsuit. And I don't want them to know until after it's resolved."

Liz could understand that. Being falsely accused was humiliating and demoralizing.

Still, it didn't mean keeping his loved ones in the dark was right. "They'd be on your side," she predicted.

Travis frowned again. "It doesn't matter. I don't want them embarrassed by any of this. And I especially don't want them to offer to help out with any of the legal expenses."

Ah, yes, money... "Why not?" Liz asked. Kelsey and Brady Anderson ran the Double Deal Ranch, one of the biggest, most successful cattle and horse operations in the state. They could easily afford it.

"Because—in their view, anyway—that would entitle them to be involved in strategy."

Liz empathized with him. She was fiercely independent by nature, too. "This is your problem. You want to solve it."

Travis nodded. "With your help."

He made it sound so personal...but why was she even considering this?

Years ago, she had fallen hard and fast for Travis. And had her heart stomped on as a result.

Now he needed her.

She should say no.

The irony of it was that she wouldn't—couldn't—turn away. Partly because she loved helping the underdog and could never resist a challenge. And Travis was that. The rest was more insidious. And deeply personal.

Now that he was back, she had to prove she'd gotten past the devastation of their breakup. That he no longer had the power to hurt her. That she had moved on to a happy, defiantly single and bulletproof life.

This was the best way.

Liz paused, sizing him up, her attorney radar on full alert. He remained all-innocence. Too innocent!

She tapped her index finger against her lips in a parody of thoughtfulness. "Why do I think you're still not telling me everything?" she asked suspiciously.

"There is one small difficulty." Travis's mouth compressed grimly. "I don't have the money to pay you."

You've got to be kidding me.

"I can compensate you monetarily for the initial consultation. Beyond that…" Travis stood and lazily ambled toward her "…I'll have to work off whatever I owe you, on this ranch."

THE FINANCIAL ARRANGEMENTS alone should have been reason enough to turn down Travis's request. Add to that the fact the two of them had once dated, albeit a very long time ago… But the bottom line was that the Four Winds bank accounts were at record lows, and he would be doing them a favor, embarking on a bartering agreement.

"You're saying I can deduct my fees from your salary," Liz ascertained, thinking how much that would help the ranch coffers.

"Until we're even. Yep."

Confident that she could easily separate the business from the personal, she held out her palm. "You've got yourself a deal."

They shook on it. Unprecedented warmth spread throughout her body as Travis's hand engulfed hers. Liz's throat went dry as she gazed up into his eyes. Maybe it wasn't going to be as easy to keep her emotional distance as she thought.

Luckily, the moment was interrupted by the loud chiming of the ranch bell.

Smiling cheerfully, she let go of his palm and stepped back. "Dinner is ready."

Travis reached for his hat and slapped it back on his head, tugging it low across his brow. "Best not keep the ladies waiting, then."

Together they slipped out of the homestead and headed past the barns to the ranch house.

"One more thing," Travis cautioned after a moment.

Liz kept moving, staying a careful distance away from him, but slanting him a curious look.

"I'd rather Tillie, Faye Elizabeth and Reba not know I've retained your services as an attorney. At least until my, uh, difficulty is all cleared up."

Thanks to the way Liz had been running off at the mouth earlier, the other Cartwright women already knew she'd suspected Travis was in some sort of downward spiral. Not that any of them seemed to care.

Liz sidestepped the opportunity to tell Travis that, and said, "I'm bound by attorney-client privilege now, as you well know. So they'll hear nothing from me about what you've just told me. But lawsuits are a matter of public record, as are the suspension of law licenses." For the second time, she warned, "This is going to get out."

He nodded, clearly aware of that. "But until it does… we'll let others assume that you and I are spending time together to go over ranch business, or reestablish our previous friendship. Agreed?"

Secrets of this sort bred an intimacy they did not need. Yet what choice did she have? Reluctantly, Liz conceded. "For now, no one else needs to know I'm representing you."

He exhaled in relief.

Bound together by the confidence, they continued walking toward the house, through the back door and into the kitchen.

"Where have you two been?" Faye Elizabeth demanded, as always on the alert for romance in Liz's life. "And why don't you have your things? I assumed that was what was taking so long at the homestead."

Not quite, Liz thought, keeping her expression bland so as not to give anything away.

Travis removed his hat and put it on a hook near the door. "That was my fault, I'm afraid." He flashed a winning smile and ran a hand through the rumpled layers of his dark brown hair. "I got to talking...."

And asking for help, Liz thought, still a little amazed he had needed it.

Clearly exasperated, Tillie herded them all toward the large, old-fashioned kitchen table—and the dinner the women had lovingly prepared. "Let them be. We've got a hot meal to eat."

And a big, strapping man to feed....

"As well as serious business to discuss," Reba added as they all sat down at the big oak table.

Travis's knee nudged Liz's as they got situated.

She flushed at the unexpected wave of heat that resulted, and edged back in her chair.

Oblivious to Liz's reaction, Reba complained, "We are way behind in the ranch work."

Liz forced herself to concentrate on something other than Travis's big, rangy frame.

"I know that, Mom." She tried not to feel as if the fate of the Four Winds was resting on her shoulders. Or would be, if she would only do what the others wanted and take over the running of the ranch, as tradition dictated. "It's why we hired Travis to help us."

Liz looked at him, hoping he would get the hint and divert their attention.

"Maybe you should make a list of what needs to be done, and in what order," he suggested with a faint smile.

While the women looked on approvingly, he placed a generous serving of tender, juicy beef brisket on his plate.

Reba passed the heaping bowl of skillet corn, livened up with diced onion and green and red pepper. "Liz can help you with that."

Liz knew a bit of ham-handed matchmaking when she saw it. She suppressed a beleaguered sigh while dishing potato salad and coleslaw onto her plate. "I think you should do it, Mom. Since you're the one running the physical side of the ranch. I'm only here when I can be, to help out."

Which wasn't all that often, given the demands of her law practice.

Reba disagreed. "I've been wanting to pass the responsibility on to you for several years now. And especially now, with my sciatica acting up again…and Travis here to do the heavy labor. It seems like it is finally time for you to take over the reins of the Four Winds."

It might seem that way to the other Cartwright women, perhaps, Liz thought with mounting resentment. Not to her.

Travis arched a brow.

"You know what to do, Liz," Reba continued persuasively. "All I'm asking is that you find time to do it."

Sidestepping the familiar argument, Liz spread a gingham napkin across her lap. She understood her duty to her family. She just couldn't do everything they wanted her to, when they wanted it done. "First things first." Trying not to notice how easily he had made himself at home in such an estrogen-charged environment, she locked eyes with Travis. "I have to clear my belongings out of the homestead so Travis can move in."

"YOU DON'T HAVE ANY intention of ever taking over management of this ranch, do you?" Travis murmured, after the meal had been concluded and the two of them had been shooed out of the ranch house and over to the homestead to get the moving done.

Just go right to the heart of things, why don't you? Liz thought.

Hating the way he saw inside her head—zeroing in on what no one else knew, even after all this time—she opened up the bureau drawers and moved her clothing into two open suitcases.

With her voice as crisp and businesslike as her actions, she continued, "It isn't necessary right now, since Great-grandma Tillie is still doing the books and the land management, Grandma Faye Elizabeth is doing the majority of the cooking and housekeeping, and my mom is overseeing most of the actual labor."

His broad shoulders flexing against the fabric of his twill work shirt, Travis boxed up Liz's books. He paused to give her a speculative once-over, then moved his gaze to her eyes. "But it will be necessary for you to manage the place eventually...."

The electricity in the room rose as surely as the intimacy.

Liz swallowed hard. It was crazy to be so aware of him.

Knowing he was waiting for her reaction, she admitted grimly, "Or end sixty-three years of Cartwright family tradition and deeply disappoint my mother, grandmother and great-grandmother."

Liz accidentally dropped a handful of undies on the floor and bent to pick them up. "Who, by the way, also want me to figure out how to have a baby and begin another generation of Cartwrights, without simultaneously having my heart broken—as all of them did, for one reason or another."

His gaze fell to the silk and lace crumpled in her palm. Travis cleared his throat. "Refresh my memory about what went down…"

"My great-grandmother was widowed when her rodeo clown husband got trampled by a bull. Faye Elizabeth lost her husband to an undiagnosed heart ailment, shortly after they married. And my mother lost my dad in a rockslide when I was just a baby." Liz sighed. "Legend has it that men who love Cartwright women never last long."

Travis scoffed. "Sounds like an old wives' tale to me."

Liz tucked her lingerie into a suitcase. "Or just plain bad luck. Besides, the Cartwright women, who have always bucked tradition and kept their surname, prefer running the ranch themselves, anyway."

He smiled. "I can see that." He walked over to help her zip up the bulging suitcases and stand them on their wheels. "Is that why you started your law practice in Laramie?"

Liz stripped the mattress and dumped the sheets into a large wicker laundry basket. She reached for a clean set and began making up the bed. Travis leaned in to help.

"I did that because I didn't like working for someone else. I worked at a midsize firm in Dallas the first three years out of law school and discovered it wasn't for me. Too many politics. Too much grunt work. Not enough autonomy." Trying not to think how intimate a task this could be, Liz tossed him a pillow and a case.

"What about you?" She remembered the way he had been in high school, all big plans and bigger ambitions.

Grinning, she speculated, "I bet you loved life in a large firm."

Then realized, too late, she probably shouldn't have said that.

After dealing with the pillow, Travis hefted the box of books in his arms. "I enjoyed the competition, the high stakes of all the clients and the cases, until I got pushed out. Then, I have to admit, it wasn't so fun."

She moved ahead of him, holding the door open. "Would you go back to it?"

He set the box in the back of her SUV. "It might be different at another big firm."

She went back to get a suitcase. Travis got the other. "So what you said earlier, about wanting your own ranch…?"

Their shoulders brushed accidentally as they reached the vehicle, causing Liz to momentarily lose her footing.

Travis put out a hand to steady her. "That's still true. I miss ranch life as much as I love the law."

She tried not to notice how ruggedly handsome he looked in the warm light of the spring evening.

They had both grown up so much in the time they had been apart.

She couldn't help but admire the man he had become. "So—unlike me—you want to do both," she ascertained quietly.

Travis went to help her carry the clothes hanging in the closet. "A lot of Texas attorneys do. Especially in the rural areas."

Liz picked up several pairs of custom cowgirl boots and the more sedate heels she wore to court. "Don't let my family hear you say that. They would use it to put additional pressure on me."

He reached over and set a flat-brimmed felt hat on her head. "They'd be right," he teased, with a confidence that let her know he had been thinking about this. "There are advantages to diversifying."

With Travis by her side, Liz made another trip to the SUV. "So where would you do this?" she asked, nearly dropping everything because she was carrying so much. "Here? In Laramie County?"

Travis draped his load of clothing over the stuff already in the back. With casual gallantry, he helped her with the mass of shoes and boots. The kind of mischief she recalled from their high school days glimmered in his eyes.

"Worried about a little competition?"

More like my heart. Although where that thought had come from... Since there was no way she was falling for him again.

Liz stepped back, aware that one more trip would just about clear out the homestead of her things. "Of course not." She tossed her hair back with the confident attitude that had gotten her through many a difficult situation. "You're an oil and gas attorney, interested in big stakes."

Wishing she was in one of her business suits instead of laid-back ranch attire of a calico shirt and jeans, she angled a thumb at her chest. "I run a general law practice that focuses on helping people with ordinary, everyday problems. When it comes right down to it, our prospective clients have as little in common as you and I do."

A brooding look crossed his face. "You're right about that," he said in a low, gravelly voice. He glanced back at the cabin. "So, are we about done here?"

Liz nodded, hating his sudden aloofness, aware she had touched a nerve without meaning to.

Tensing with regret, she handed him the keys to the homestead and shifted the conversation back to business. "When do you want to get started giving me the background information on the lawsuit against you?"

Travis did not miss a beat. "How about tonight?"

Chapter Three

An hour and a half later, tensions were high. And so, Travis thought, were his emotions.

"Do you want me to help you or not?" Liz demanded, her frustration with him apparent.

Travis figured she would be a hard-charging advocate. It was the reason he had hired her. It did not mean, however, that he wanted to bare his soul, to her or anyone else. He sat back in his chair and regarded her with unchecked irritation, taking in her upswept auburn hair. "How my relationship with Olympia started is irrelevant to the case."

Bracing her hands on her desktop, Liz leaned toward him. She looked at him as if she could read him right down to the marrow of his soul and was not exactly thrilled with what she found.

She arched an elegant eyebrow and moved around to stand in front of the desk. "I will decide what's relevant and what is not." She stared at him with lawyerly intensity, then enunciated slowly, "Your job, as my client, is to answer my questions as openly and honestly as possible."

Telling himself he could handle her, even in full battle mode, Travis added, "And stop thinking like an attorney while I'm at it, right?" He was beginning to see what made her so formidable in and out of the courtroom.

"It would help." Frowning, Liz picked up the legal documents he had brought for her to peruse. "I don't need you second-guessing me."

Then what did she need?

Not that he wanted to go there. Especially with the trouble he was in.

Travis slouched in his chair, reluctantly returning his mind to business. "That's not what I was doing."

Liz looked down her nose at him in rigid disagreement. "You're trying to run the defense." As if finding it difficult to be that physically close to him, she abruptly straightened and moved away. "And you of all people ought to know better, because 'a man who is his own lawyer has a fool for his client.'"

Much as he wanted to, Travis could not argue with that. He sighed and glanced around Liz's law office. Unlike the ultra-luxurious one he'd had at Haverty, Brockman & Roberts, this one was sparsely decorated, with beige walls, sturdy dark wood furniture and comfortable client chairs. The focal point here was Liz. With her hair twisted into a casual knot at the nape of her neck, her attitude unerringly focused and businesslike, she was clearly in her element.

She belonged here, Travis thought. Not working the ranch.

She picked up the yellow legal pad she'd been writing on moments earlier and settled herself in her chair. "Now, back to the beginning…" she continued.

Travis tried not to groan.

"How—and under what circumstances—did you and Olympia Herndon meet?"

Not as accidentally as I thought. "I met her at a charity function we were both attending. I'd heard she was looking for new representation. Before I could approach her, she introduced herself to me."

Liz scribbled furiously. "Did you talk about her search?"

"Not that evening, no. We just got to know each other a little bit."

Tapping her pen impatiently on the pad, Liz prompted, "And then what?"

Already restless, Travis stood and prowled her office, inspecting the art—mostly black-and-white photographs of the Four Winds—on the wall. "I saw her again…socially…at a dinner party given by the senior partners and their wives. And then at another fundraiser." He spun around. Lounging against a bookcase, he thrust his hands in the pockets of his jeans. "A few weeks later, I started representing her." Aware that if they kept up the conversation they could be headed into dangerous territory, he compressed his lips. "Why does any of this matter?"

"Because Ms. Herndon is asserting in her lawsuit that you did not provide adequate, competent representation or act as a zealous advocate on her behalf."

Fury gathered in his gut. He hated being put in the position of having to defend himself. "I did everything possible to get that wildcatter to sign with her company. He just didn't want to."

Liz studied him. "Would he testify to that?"

Travis wondered if the skin of her face was as silky-soft as it looked. Ditto for her lips.

He shrugged. "I don't know. Digger Dobbs doesn't strike me as somebody who wants to get involved in somebody else's mess."

Liz twisted her lips. Making him wonder if she still

kissed the way she once had—like an innocent virgin who preferred to keep her heart under lock and key.

"Well, he's at the center of this so we're going to have to contact him." She paused as her cell phone began to ring, and glanced at the caller ID. "Sorry. This is the Laramie County Sheriff's Department. I've got to get it." She picked up. "Liz Cartwright. Yeah, hi, Rio. What? You're kidding! No. Heck, no! Tell him I'll be right there!"

She clicked off the phone, already half out of her seat. "Client emergency. I've got to go."

Irked to be put on hold, Travis rose. "What about—"

Liz flashed by. "We'll pick it up later. Even tonight if you want. Right now, I have to get over to Spring Street before J. T. Haskell lands himself in jail."

TRAVIS HEADED OUT THE DOOR after her. "J. T. Haskell is your client?"

Liz cast a look at the dusky sky. The sun had slipped past the horizon, and it would be dark soon. "I have a habit of taking on underdogs."

Travis nodded. "So it would seem," he retorted drily.

Liz slanted him a glance while locking up. Having a big-shot attorney for a client was going to be harder than she'd thought. Partly because he was reluctant to relinquish control, and partly because she had the gut feeling there was still a lot he wasn't telling her. Things she needed to know to adequately represent him.

But that was no surprise. Clients never gave their attorney all the information up front. Usually because they were trying to maintain their dignity, garner respect. It was up to counsel to retrieve all the facts and get to the bottom line.

Even when it came to defending another attorney.

Liz sighed. As they headed toward the parking lot, she turned the conversation back to the matter at hand. "Why are you so surprised I'm representing J.T.?"

Travis shrugged. "I heard he went off the deep end after his wife died last year."

An understatement if there ever was one. "He kind of has," she admitted with a grimace.

"He's been arrested a couple of times for bar fights."

"Actually, he was just busting up some furniture. He wasn't drunk and he didn't hit anyone. But, yeah, there are a number of places he can't go in now because of his bad behavior."

"Anyone talked to him about joining one of Kate Marten-McCabe's grief groups over at the hospital?"

Liz's frustration spiraled. "Everyone has."

"He's not buying it?"

"He doesn't think he has a problem."

Travis stopped at her SUV, all protective male. "I'm going with you."

The firmness of his voice was a surprise.

Travis was quiet a moment, just looking at her with those keen eyes that seemed to see more than she liked. "He's a big guy. If he's upset, he could be dangerous."

Liz attempted to curtail her irritation. Since when did she need protecting—from anyone? Well used to looking after her own interests, she said, "The sheriff's department is on the way."

Travis flashed an easygoing smile and climbed in the passenger side. "Consider it part of my new duties, protecting all the women on the Cartwright ranch."

Maybe it was her imagination, but it felt a little more than that. "I hate to tell you this, cowboy." She got in after him and slid her key in the ignition. "But we're not on the Four Winds."

He shrugged and turned to pull the safety restraint out of its sheath. "You know what I mean."

She did. And she didn't have time to argue. "Fine." Liz put on her shoulder belt, too, then sent him a warning glare. "Just don't put on your lawyer hat. This is my situation to handle."

By the time they got to the Haskell home on Spring Street, the streetlamps were on and the sheriff's car was already there. Deputies Rio Vasquez and Kyle McCabe were in the front yard, which, given the many stakes and flags, looked as if it had recently been surveyed.

Bypassing the crowd of neighbors who had gathered, Liz marched into the center of the circle of men. Not exactly the best way to spend a tranquil spring evening. "What's going on?"

Tim Patrone pointed to Haskell. "J.T. has gone too far, that's what is going on."

The recently retired man glowered, his face red beneath his shock of white hair. "I want to take down a few trees and build a lagoon-style pool with a waterfall. What's wrong with that?"

"In the front yard!" Tim retorted.

Liz took in J.T.'s tropical shirt, flip-flops and walking shorts. "I know you have a reason for doing what you're doing."

He rubbed the stubble of a three-day-old beard. "Don't I always?"

"Suppose you tell everyone here what it is." *Before real trouble erupts.*

"Cyndi, God bless her soul, always wanted to go to Hawaii. And I never did take her. I figure this is the least I can do. Besides, I offered to let all the neighborhood kids swim in it, once it's built, so I don't see what the big deal is."

"And that's another big problem. Safety!" Tim fumed.

Deputy Vasquez intervened. "Local ordinance requires a six-foot barrier around any private swimming pool."

"Then I'll put one up," J.T. said with a shrug.

The neighbors appeared outraged at the idea. Liz understood why. A six-foot privacy fence in the front yard would ruin the look of all the homes on the street, as well as obstruct the view.

Liz moved forward and put a hand on J.T.'s arm. "There are zoning considerations, too. You're going to need a permit to proceed. And I doubt the town of Laramie will grant you one for a swimming pool in the front yard, no matter how beautiful or lavish it is."

"Well, there's not room in the backyard," J.T. declared. "Not for what I want to do."

"Then buy a place in the country and move it all out there!" Tim advised.

J.T. flushed all the more. "I am not giving up the home I shared with my late wife. All our memories are here."

No one could argue with that. Cyndi and J.T. had been inseparable until the day she died.

Before her client could say anything else, Liz intervened again. Her voice soothing, she looked at him and murmured, "J.T., you and I need to talk about this. Let's go inside."

"Nope," he said. He put his hands in front of him and glared at the two deputies. "I don't want your visit to be wasted. You want to arrest me for disturbing the peace? Arrest me!"

Rio and Kyle exchanged beleaguered looks.

"Or do I have to hit something first?" J.T. taunted,

picking up one of the staked flags, clearly ready to make good on his claim.

"That's it." Rio got out his handcuffs before J.T. could snap the stake in half. "You're going to a holding cell to cool off."

"Whatever." He let them take the stake from him. "I'm still building the pool!" He glared at his neighbors defiantly, still spoiling for a fight. "And no one is going to stop me!"

A pitying silence fell.

J.T. looked at Liz as he was led away, hands cuffed behind him. "You want to do something?" he shouted over his brawny shoulder. "Get me a permit so I can build this pool!"

"He's losing it," Travis said as they got back in Liz's car and followed the squad car to the sheriff's station.

"He's grieving. He loved his wife so much. To see Cyndi lose her battle with lung disease was more than he could bear. He has to have some outlet for his anger."

"Meaning what?" Travis scoffed. "You think he should be able to follow through on his crazy plan and, while he's at it, lower the property values of every house on the street?"

"It's not about building a pool. It's about paying tribute to his wife, lamenting his loss and getting over his guilt for all the things he didn't give Cyndi. He wants her back, Travis." *He wants the love he lost.* "He wants to rewrite the past, and he can't do that, so he's ticked off. I get it."

A long silence fell. "You really feel for the guy."

Liz forced herself to concentrate on driving, instead of on the handsome man in the passenger seat beside her. "I've always had a thing for the underdog, in any situation. You know that."

"I'm not sure I'd call J.T. an underdog," Travis countered quietly.

Liz frowned at the red light, her foot on the brake pedal. "He's at a disadvantage because of his distraught emotional state. He's picking battles no one in their right mind would ever expect him to win."

"Which is why you're so drawn to him," Travis concluded as the light changed and the SUV began to move again. "Because you think you can claim victory."

Feeling the heat of his gaze like a physical caress, Liz turned at the next street. "Not in the sense of getting him a tropical haven in his front yard. But if I could help him put his life back on track, and keep him out of serious legal trouble in the meantime, I'd be happy."

Travis didn't take his eyes off her. "You really care about him."

Liz was suddenly feeling a little too aware of Travis. "I do. And I owe him." She turned into a parking spot, cut the engine and turned to Travis in all sincerity. "A few years ago, my mom and grandmother were driving a truck full of baby calves to a ranch thirty miles north of the Four Winds when the truck broke down unexpectedly. It was a brutally hot day. They were out in the middle of nowhere. And there was nowhere they could safely put the cattle while they went for help. Nor could they just leave them in the blistering interior of the cattle car...."

She drew a deep breath, shook her head. "Angels must have been looking down on them, because right then J.T. drove by. He was on his way to a job himself—as a satellite installer—but he stopped to help. Not only did he get another cattle truck out there within minutes, he helped transfer the calves and then stayed with our truck until the tow service arrived. Had he not been there, had he not known just who in that particular area to call for help, we might have had a very different outcome." Liz paused to let her words sink in. "J.T. is a good guy. He's just going through a rough patch."

Travis studied her, a combination of respect and admiration on his handsome face. "He's lucky to have you in his corner."

Liz warmed at the compliment. "Let's just hope I can do something for him."

"No WAY," RIO VASQUEZ SAID. "He's spending the night in a holding cell. He can go in front of the judge in the morning."

Liz squared off with the arresting officers. "Guys, come on.…"

Kyle McCabè stood firm, too. "It's for his own good. Besides, you saw him, Liz. J.T. was practically pleading with us to bring him in."

Maybe, Liz thought, so he wouldn't have to spend another night alone in the house he had shared with his beloved Cyndi.

Travis put a hand on her shoulder. "They're right."

Liz knew it. She just didn't want to admit that everything she had said to J.T. about his behavior so far had been ineffective. She lifted a hand. "Fine. I'll be back first thing tomorrow." The hours in between would give her time to think about what she wanted to say to the judge.

Travis and Liz walked out of the sheriff's station. "So what now?" he asked, suddenly looking almost as restless as she felt.

She consulted her watch. It was only nine-thirty.

"It's Friday evening," Travis continued. "Do you

have somewhere you need to be? Someone you need to see?"

His lack of subtlety was not lost on her.

He was trying to figure her out, the same way she'd been trying to get a handle on him. And his current legal problem.

Figuring it might help convince him to confide in her if they lightened up a little, she allowed herself to tease him back. "Why, Counselor, are you asking me if I have a date?"

He grinned at her exaggerated Texas accent. "I didn't see any photos of a boyfriend at your office." He paused, his eyes opaque. "Or the homestead, for that matter."

Liz let out a long, careful breath. She slowed her steps, delaying the moment they would get back into her SUV. Suddenly, the space felt a tad too intimate.

She lifted her chin. "That's because I don't have one."

"Which means what?" His eyes narrowed, he stepped close enough that she could smell the leather-and-soap scent of his hair and skin. "You're not dating?" He reached up to tuck a strand of her hair behind her ear. "You're opposed to dating?"

When she didn't answer, he met her gaze. "It's nothing I couldn't easily find out from someone else. I just thought…" His voice dropped another notch, in a way that sent heat slashing through her. "If the story is that we're resuming our friendship, we ought to know the basic facts about each other."

The woman in her wanted to keep up all the barriers. The attorney in her knew he was right. Plus, she was curious about him, too.

She resumed walking toward the parking lot behind

the sheriff's station while gazing up at the stars shimmering in the black velvet sky above. "I had a serious relationship a few years ago, when I was working in Dallas." She shook off the unhappy memories. "We broke off our engagement by mutual agreement."

Travis cocked his head and ran his gaze over her like a caress. "Are you still friends?"

"Not really." She rummaged in her pocket for her keys, then hit the electronic keypad. The locks clicked; the interior lights went on. "It's kind of hard to come back from something like that."

He opened the driver's door for her, stood waiting for her to get in. "And since…?"

The intensity of his regard had her whole body tensing. Liz adapted the casual attitude that perfectly summed up her nonexistent love life, the one that had the women in the family so worried she would never fall in love, never marry, never have a baby to carry on the Cartwright bloodline. "I've had the occasional date here and there." She forced herself to meet his probing gaze. "What about you?"

He shrugged. It was, Liz thought, his turn to skillfully evade.

"I'd like to date. In theory. I just never seem to have the time."

A lament voiced by many an associate at big law firms. "Not part of your one-, five- and ten-year plans?"

"Actually, marriage and family is. If I could ever figure out where I would work it in."

That was a surprise, Liz thought. Travis had been so focused on his career, she hadn't expected this was something he would want. She sized him up, wondering which allure would turn out to be stronger, his desire to live a more authentic, not so big-city life, or his desire to redeem his name and regain his former glory. "So when this is over, you plan to go back to working eighty-hour weeks…."

He shrugged, not about to commit yet, either way. "It is the norm for an associate in any big or midsize law firm," he offered casually. "No matter where it is located."

Liz knew that.

Lawyers in Lubbock who wanted fame and fortune—and the bank accounts that went with them—worked as hard as attorneys in Houston.

Fortunately, she had learned there were other, more important things in life.

Like feeling you made a difference.

She bit her lip, admitting, "Too many long hours are exactly why I quit my job at that firm in Dallas. I wanted more of a life outside the office."

"And yet," he murmured, playfully tapping the end of her nose, "here you are at 9:45 on a Friday night… lamenting your lack of a love life, same as me."

Liz stiffened. Honestly, the man was taking far too much for granted. "I didn't say I missed it," she returned archly. *Even if I have been wondering all evening long just how it would feel to kiss you….*

"Really." He lifted his eyebrows and waited for her gaze to meet his.

Indignation flushing her cheeks, Liz asserted, "I can live without sex." Could he?

Travis grinned, as if he would like nothing more than to wear her down. "How about this?" he asked her softly. Grasping her waist, he tugged her against him. Threaded one hand through her hair, tilting her face to his. His mouth lowered seductively. "Can you live without a kiss?"

Chapter Four

Her mouth went dry. The practical side of Liz said *Don't kiss him.* The romantic side of her insisted there was no harm in finding out if Travis Anderson still had the power to take her breath away as he had back in high school.

So instead of rebuffing him, she stepped into the fray. Allowed him to keep right on coming and lower his mouth to hers.

The first touch of their lips was astonishing. Electric. And oh so sweet. The first hint of subtle pressure was even more intoxicating.

Before Liz knew it, she had surrendered to the moment and moved all the way into his embrace. Her breasts brushed the hardness of his chest and her arms slipped around him.

Travis moved forward, too, sliding his palms down her hips and holding her against his body. Her softness melded to his strength and the kiss took on a quiet intensity that turned her whole world upside down.

Liz moaned, tilting her head to give him better access, relishing the sure sweep of his tongue tangling with hers.

She knew she had wanted him years ago, even if

they were too young, too reserved, too focused on everything else to fully explore that yearning.

Turns out, the schoolgirl passion she'd experienced back then was nothing compared to what she felt now that they were all grown up.

Holding him like this, letting him hold her, was magic. And she knew if they kept it up—if they let this recklessly wild kiss continue—there would be nothing but regrets for both of them.

Shuddering, she clasped his shoulders and pushed him away. "We can't do this."

"Actually," Travis teased, kissing her temple, her cheek, the lobe of her ear, "I think we were excelling in this venue...."

With her body still tingling everywhere they had touched—and everywhere they hadn't—Liz took another step back and tried to regain her composure. "You're my client." She emphasized every syllable of every word.

He grinned sexily, not at all repentant. "Lucky for me. It's the one good thing, besides a temporary job, I've got going for me at the moment."

That was Travis all right, Liz thought in exasperation. Charging headlong into whatever awaited. Letting nothing stand between him and his goal.

Her heart racing, she tried again to talk sense into him. "We were kissing." She held up a hand before he could interrupt. "And you and I both know that crossing the line this way will lead to nothing but trouble."

His expression solemn, he gazed at her. "I agree," he told her in a husky voice. "If we let this impact the way we conduct ourselves in terms of the business at hand, it will bring us bucketfuls of heartache. But that's not going to happen over a kiss, Liz." He leaned closer, his breath fanning her neck. "And you know why? Because we're both lawyers. And we're smart enough to be able to separate our private lives from our professional alliances."

She had certainly thought that was the case up till now.

She'd never even been tempted before. But Travis had thrown her emotions into chaos, by kissing her for just a few minutes.

Deliberately, she put her lawyer hat back on. "Which makes our actions all the more foolish," she retorted. "You have to know that."

His gray eyes darkened. He looked a little bemused, and a lot cocky. "Actually," he drawled, letting his gaze drift slowly over her face, "if you want to get technical—and it sounds like you do—there's nothing in the Texas Bar Ethics Code or Texas law preventing me from having a relationship with you outside of your work on the lawsuit. Besides—" he shrugged, still not ready to give up on pursuing her "—with you at the helm, this case will be over before you know it."

Liz appreciated Travis's faith in her even as she worried that her success meant he would soon be leaving Laramie County.

Wishing her lips weren't still tingling, she looked him straight in the eye. "That doesn't mean it's wise for us to revisit past mistakes. We've been down this road before."

"As kids."

Past hurt rushed to the fore. That didn't mean they hadn't crashed and burned. Or that she hadn't felt incredibly dejected and cried into her pillow for weeks afterward.

Her lower lip trembled. "You broke up with me, Travis."

He stood there, patient and ready, raring to turn back the clock. "Because there was too much of an age difference." Exasperation colored his low tone. He tucked a strand of hair behind her ear. "And we weren't right for each other then."

"We're still not." She stepped back, not about to put her heart on the line, only to have it smashed to pieces. Again. "So let me be clear." She slayed him with her best don't-mess-with-me look. "I'm very happy to represent you. I'm glad you will be temporarily assisting my family and working on the Four Winds. But that, Counselor, is as far as it goes."

"At least let me send you off with a cup of coffee and a couple of breakfast tacos," Faye Elizabeth insisted at six the next morning.

Studiously ignoring the big male interloper sitting at the breakfast table, Liz simultaneously pulled on her suit jacket and checked her BlackBerry for messages.

She'd been up half the night, revisiting his kiss and her response to it, as well as everything that had happened years ago.

Travis, on the other hand, looked like he had slept great.

It figured.

She forced a smile and an attitude of nonchalance. "That would be wonderful." Liz gave her grandmother a hug. "Thank you."

Reba frowned, looking from Travis to her daughter and back again.

"What's going on with the two of you?" she asked.

He kissed me and I responded, Liz thought. *My goodness, how I responded...*

It was a wonder she hadn't melted into a puddle right there in the parking lot.

But not about to tell her family that, she shrugged, accepting with a murmur of thanks the breakfast her grandmother had packed. "I don't know what you're talking about," Liz fibbed.

"Something happened," Tillie concurred, a matchmaker's gleam in her eyes.

"And why were the two of you in town together last night, anyway?" Reba pressed.

"How did you hear that?" Travis asked.

Liz had heard him say he had gone off to get his belongings. Which he had eventually done, after collecting his vehicle.

"One of my friends saw the two of you coming out of your office, late in the evening," Reba declared.

Small towns. Nary a secret anywhere. At least that's how it seemed....

"I want Travis to sign a temporary employment contract with the Four Winds," Liz said, in all honesty.

He looked at her, in lawyer mode, as able to roll with the punches as she hoped. "I think it's a good idea, too."

Faye Elizabeth regarded them suspiciously. "You couldn't have done that here?"

Clearly, she hoped to keep them apart, or well chaperoned as much as possible to prevent any further romance from developing.

"It's easier doing business in my office," Liz said.

Especially with all three other Cartwright women looking over their shoulders, speculating on what was and wasn't happening between her and Travis.

"Unfortunately," Travis interjected with a beleaguered smile, "Liz had an emergency with another client that called her away, and we didn't finish. So we'll have to go back to it at some point soon."

They would, Liz realized reluctantly. Which would mean even more time spent alone with him.

Only this time there would be no kissing. She would make certain of it.

"That won't keep you from checking the new calves in the pastures this morning, will it, Travis?" Reba asked in alarm.

"Not at all." He finished his coffee and stood. "I'll get right on it. Thanks for the fine breakfast. Ladies…" He grabbed his hat and strolled out.

"My oh my," Tillie sighed, her hand fluttering above her heart.

"I quite agree," Reba said, sizing up his departing image the same way she sized up the procreating powers of a bull for hire. "Having a man like that for your baby's daddy…"

"Mom!" Liz said, flushing hotly.

"I'm just saying…." Reba eyed her matter-of-factly, in that instant every bit as goal-oriented as Travis. "You're not getting any younger and we need a new generation of Cartwrights. Travis is here. He's hot. He's available."

"Why not just go ahead and say it—he's a stud!" Liz interrupted sarcastically.

"And he's from prime breeding stock," Reba continued, without skipping a beat. She lifted a palm. "The two of you wouldn't even have to marry—"

"Of course they would marry," Tillie exclaimed, her romantic sensibilities offended by the notion of them having a baby and not living happily ever after.

"A romance with a man who's not going to stick

around for the long haul is the last thing Liz needs," Faye Elizabeth grumbled.

Tired of having her life decided for her, by everyone *but* her, Liz sighed and grabbed her briefcase and her breakfast. "I'm out of here," she told one and all grouchily.

To her consternation, by the time she reached the parking area, Travis's pickup truck was disappearing down a dirt road that traversed the ranch.

Figuring she could talk to him later, she headed for the Laramie County sheriff's station.

"You have to stop picking fights with people," Liz told J.T. when they met up in the courtroom.

Disheveled and exhausted from a night spent in the holding cell, he remained defiant. "People," he returned cantankerously, "need to stop waging battles with me."

"This isn't what your late wife would want for you."

He ignored her reference to his beloved Cyndi. "I want that pool." He peered at Liz. "And I know you can figure out a way for it to happen."

Talk about the impossible.

She sighed.

"Meantime, if I get community service for this, make sure it's something outside," J.T. continued. "I hate being cooped up."

Liz tried another approach. "You don't have to plead guilty to the misdemeanor charges. I can get them dropped if you'll only agree to get some grief counseling."

J.T. scowled. "You know how I feel about that."

"Nothing is going to make your grief go away, I know," Liz repeated his oft-muttered sentiment.

"Exactly."

Figuring that, under the circumstances, community

service couldn't hurt, since it would get him out of the house, Liz did as he asked.

The guilty plea was entered; he was lectured by the exasperated judge and assigned twenty hours of community service cleaning up local streets.

An hour later, she was headed back to the office.

It was noon by the time she arrived at the ranch.

Pale gray clouds were obscuring the horizon. Reba, Tillie and Faye Elizabeth were in the midst of gathering up their purses—and raincoats, just in case.

"What's going on?" Liz asked. Given the fact it was a Saturday, they could be headed anywhere.

Tillie stuffed her notepad and pen in her handbag. Reba grabbed the keys to her own SUV. "We're making our monthly shopping trip to the warehouse club in San Angelo."

Liz wished she'd had more notice. Not having any destroyed her ability to adequately adjust her own workload. Nevertheless, she had a responsibility here. "Give me a couple of minutes and I'll go with you."

"That would be great!" her grandmother said. "We'll wait while you change clothes."

Reba gave her mother a chiding look, then turned back to Liz. "Actually, honey, we need you here, helping Travis move the cattle from pasture 53 to 62."

With ten thousand acres of ranch land and only some of it currently fit for grazing, moving cattle around could be quite a task.

To her consternation, Tillie quickly reinforced that sentiment. "I don't care how good Travis is on horseback, he can't do it alone, dear. Well, not efficiently, anyway. Not with all the newborn calves and their mamas."

"I'd do it myself if my hip were up to getting in the saddle," Reba said.

Liz knew that to be true. There was nothing her mother liked more than cowgirl activities.

Liz ignored Faye Elizabeth's lingering disapproval. There was no use aggravating her mother's sciatica when it was just starting to mend. "Of course I'll help with the cattle," Liz said. She turned to Faye Elizabeth. "You don't need to worry. I can handle Travis."

Her grandmother harrumphed. "See that you do."

Through discussing her love life—or lack thereof—Liz continued, practically, "When will you-all be back?"

"Around dinnertime, if all goes as planned…"

The ladies took off, and Liz went up to change clothes. Grimly, she downed an energy bar, saddled up and headed out.

Travis was where they'd said he would be, in pasture 53. He was hardly alone.

Reins in hand, she cantered over to join him. "Who are your buddies?"

They hadn't had ranch dogs for some time.

These two were beauties.

Mutts, to be sure, but gorgeous ones. Both fast and agile as could be.

"Meet Mud." Travis pointed to the smaller one. He had a thick brown-white-and-black coat and looked to be part border collie, part beagle. "And Jet." He indicated a glossy black Labrador retriever–German shepherd mix.

"Hey, fellas." Liz smiled from her place in the saddle.

"I borrowed them from my parents' ranch," Travis said. "They've got about two dozen cattle dogs out there, so we can keep them as long as we want them. What brings you out here?"

"I was told you needed help moving cattle."

His expression didn't change in the slightest. Yet there was something in his gray eyes. Some small glimmer of bemusement...

Liz stifled a moan. "They knew you had the dogs helping you, didn't they?"

Which made her assistance unnecessary, as there were only seventy-five mama cows, with fifty baby calves to date. A lot for Liz's mom to handle on her own, but nothing for a cowhand as fit and experienced as Travis. Especially when he was accompanied by two well-trained herding dogs.

He shrugged lazily in response to her question. "Introductions were made. Plans announced."

Liz bit down on an oath. "Tillie and my mom are matchmaking."

"But not Faye Elizabeth."

Liz shrugged. "Of all of us, she's the one who worries the most. So, you take that, plus her past—growing up without a dad, losing her husband so quickly after they married then watching my mom lose hers—I just don't think she can bear to see any of us experience that kind of heartbreak again."

"Whereas Tillie..." Travis prodded.

"Is still deeply romantic."

"And your mom?"

"Practical to a fault." To the point Reba was angling to make Travis Liz's baby daddy. But Travis didn't need to know that.

His eyes gleamed. "I figured it was something like that." Again, he wasn't the least upset.

Liz swallowed. It didn't matter how sexy he looked in

the saddle with a cowboy hat pulled low over his brow. She was his lawyer; he was a ranch employee. Their agreement specified nothing about social activities between them. And for good reason. Their lives were already complicated enough.

Liz grabbed the reins and wheeled her horse around. "As long as I'm here, let's get to it."

The next hour was spent cutting the mama cows and their calves from the herd. While Jet and Mud ran back and forth, barking and chasing the cattle toward the gates, Travis and Liz sorted those with calves into pasture 62, the still-gestating cows into pasture 54.

Once finished, they met up again, the dogs trotting happily alongside.

Travis settled his hat more squarely on his head. "I know the ranch isn't your deal, that you're not actually running the show, but…got time to look at a few things?"

Hating the ominous undertone in his voice, Liz nodded. Duty called once again. "Sure."

Travis took the lead. On the southernmost part of the ranch, a dozen pastures were in bad shape. Grass was sparse, weeds prevalent.

"My guess is these were grazed too short in dry conditions last summer," he said, "limiting the carbohydrate reserves that fuel spring growth."

Guiltily, Liz recalled Tillie harping on the way the cattle had been moved—or not—the previous summer. Her mother had insisted that Liz be around to saddle up and help out more, but she hadn't been able to, due to the demands of her law practice.

Reba had eventually given up nagging and done what she could, with occasional hired help.

"At this point in the spring, the grass should be green and thick," Liz mused.

Travis nodded. "Ideally, now that it's not necessary to give the herd supplemental feed and nutrients, as we do in winter, we should put them in fields where the growth is six inches tall. Let them graze it down three inches or so, and move them again. Quick rotation of the herd in spring will help a pasture recover, while preventing grasses from flowering and losing forage quality."

Liz clasped the horn on her saddle while her horse danced restlessly. "Great-grandma Tillie is always saying that spring grazing is all about management."

"She's right." Travis turned his horse in the direction of the ranch house. With a nod of his head, he indicated Liz should follow. "Fortunately, it can be fixed with fertilizer, rain and regular mowing."

All of which Travis could do.

He cantered on ahead, letting his horse—and the dogs—stretch their legs to their hearts' content.

"I was serious about getting you to sign a temporary work agreement," Liz said, after they'd taken care of their mounts and put their tack away.

Travis stood in the shadow of the barn, a resting dog on either side of him. "I've been working on something I want to show you, too," he said.

Liz glanced at her watch. It was nearly five. Where had the time gone? And why did she suddenly feel so happy and content?

She waited for Travis to elaborate, but he didn't.

Given how seriously he was taking his position as ranch hand, it was probably something about the Four Winds. Questions about why they had such a small herd these days, or some such thing.

"We probably don't have a lot of time before the others get back," Liz warned. Just this once, she'd like to get whatever news there was about the running of the ranch first. "What do you say we both shower and meet up at the ranch house around six? We can talk while we eat."

Travis nodded, his face suddenly inscrutable.

A tingle slid down her spine at his sudden shift in mood.

"See you in a little while," he said.

Liz watched his retreating back, wondering what he was up to.

Chapter Five

"Do you want the good news first?" Liz asked the moment Travis walked in the back door to the kitchen, file folder in hand.

Damn but she was pretty fresh out of the shower, in a pair of dark, boot-cut jeans and a ruffled, ivory, button-up shirt. She smelled good, too, like jasmine and shampoo.

He strolled closer, taking in the fall of auburn hair bouncing against her slender shoulders, the gentle rise and fall of her breasts. Refusing to let his gaze go any lower, he set the folder he carried on the kitchen table and followed her into the mudroom to the upright freezer.

"Or the bad news?" Liz finished with a wry smile.

His eyes stayed on her lush, kissable lips. No contest. "The good."

Liz opened the freezer and perused the contents thoughtfully, finally reaching for a butcher-paper-wrapped package with "rib eye" scrawled across it.

She shut the door with her hip and brushed by him, the heels of her fancy burgundy cowgirl boots tapping purposefully across the oak floor. "The rest of my family won't be back until around nine-thirty."

"So we've got plenty of time to go over the employment contract I drew up," she continued, looking more relaxed than he'd seen her.

Wondering how he could help, Travis watched her put the steak into the microwave to defrost. "What's the bad news?"

She made a mournful sound and pressed the heel of her hand to her forehead in a parody of misery. "We're on our own for dinner."

Travis chuckled at her antics. "And that's bad because...?"

Sober green eyes met his. "I'm not anywhere near the cook my grandmother is."

Who cared? The company alone made the evening worthwhile. Travis edged closer. "I think we'll survive."

Liz's eyes twinkled. "You say that now..."

He rolled up the sleeves on his chambray shirt. "Tell me what I can do."

She wrinkled her nose and gave him a teasing once-over. "I thought you said you can't cook."

"I can't." Travis tried not to think about her touching him every place her eyes had been. He lounged against the counter, hands braced on either side of him. "But I can follow directions—sort of."

She grinned at the understatement and went over to get the paperwork she'd prepared. "I'll man the stove. You read through these."

While Travis perused the printed pages, Liz got the meat out of the microwave and set a heavy cast-iron skillet on a burner to heat.

Travis reviewed the proffered terms. "You're requiring only twenty-four hours' notice if I decide to quit—which I can do at any time?"

She nodded, her mouth as abruptly sober as her gaze. "We hired you on short notice. I figure you should be able to leave the same way. Which I assume you will want to do as soon as we get your situation resolved."

A few hours ago Travis would have agreed that would be the case. But that had been before he'd spent the afternoon on horseback, chasing cows with Liz.

"'Room and board is supplied in full,'" he read out loud, "'in addition to a salary of four thousand a month, minus any outstanding legal fees.'"

Liz drizzled olive oil into the skillet, adding a couple tablespoons of butter, then eyed him over her shoulder. "The language in the contract's okay with you?" The steaks hit the pan with a satisfying sizzle.

Not surprised to find her as generous as ever, Travis nodded and signed. "Now take a look at what I drew up for you." Their fingers touched as he handed her the file.

"A prerelationship contract?" she asked in disbelief.

Travis didn't just set goals; he believed in hedging his bets whenever and wherever possible. "Sometimes called a 'love contract' by human resource departments. Or in our case," he allowed softly, "a predating agreement."

"Hmm. Precedent setting. At least on the Four Winds Ranch!" She read on, pausing to turn the steaks before they started to burn. "Basically, this says any relationship we should choose to have is of our free will and hence will not impact our work with each other in any way."

Judging by her expression, just reading the words made her feel better. Which had been Travis's intent.

"Right." He grabbed a chair and spun it around, straddling it. "If we do decide to go down that road, and it doesn't work out, there is no legal remedy to be had. I can't sue you. You can't sue me. Neither of us can say we were blindsided by anything that does or does not develop, because signing this document establishes that we had a past relationship. And have already shared one kiss."

A kiss that had rocked his world.

And hers—if the look in her eyes immediately after had been any indication.

A reluctant smile flickered on her lips. "It's a nifty little insurance policy, I'll hand you that," she admitted.

"One that will protect both of us, in the event anything happens. Or—" Travis paused, carefully weighting his words "—nothing else does."

WAS THAT WHAT SHE WANTED to happen? Liz wondered a little unsteadily. Nothing? Or was she already hovering on the brink, wishing they could go back, go forward, go somewhere that would leave her feeling less unsettled than she did now?

The scent of slightly charred meat teased her nostrils.

Realizing their dinner would go up in flames unless she did something, she grabbed a fork and lifted the steaks onto a plate. Covering them with foil and setting them aside, she turned off the burner, then added a quarter cup of whiskey to deglaze the pan. When the brown bits had been scooped up and the liquid evaporated, she poured in beef stock and motioned him over as she turned the burner back on low. "Could you stir this for me, please?"

"Sure." His hand nudged hers as he took the wooden spoon. An awkward silence fell. "So you're okay with the predating disclosure agreement?" he asked.

Liz picked up a pen and signed on the line reserved for her. The lawyer in her knew he was just being practical and going the extra mile to protect—and reassure—them both. "It's a good idea. Thanks for drafting the document." Finished, she handed him the pen and watched him sign the document, too. Going to the fridge, she brought out the leftover skillet corn and a head of lettuce.

Wordlessly, he stirred as she cut thick wedges and drizzled them with ranch dressing. She realized she wasn't the only one keeping her own counsel.

"I don't want you to think I'm making assumptions," Travis said eventually. "I just want us to be able to feel comfortable moving forward."

That would be easy, with all liability out of the way. Liz walked back to the stove and added a dash of cream to the simmering broth.

"I know…and I appreciate it," she replied, with the same professional calm, glad they were both thinking and acting like lawyers again. It was a heck of a lot better than behaving like lovestruck teens, making out on the street in plain view of anyone who might pass by.

"So, back to concentrating on the malpractice charges. I'm going to need copies of all the emails and letters you sent to Olympia and to Digger Dobbs regarding the business deal that fell through," Liz said as they sat down at the table with their meal.

Travis cut into his steak. "I'll put it together for you."

"Did you keep a journal?"

The sauce-covered meat melted in his mouth. "No."

"Meeting notes?"

"Yes. I followed up everything with a memo."

"Great." Liz forked up her own steak with gusto. "What about to-do lists?"

"I have some on my personal computer, but they're

cryptic. I'm not sure my shorthand to myself will hold up in court."

Her gaze met his. "That's okay. We can use them to bolster your recollections and help reconstruct."

Liz looked up at the sound of a vehicle rumbling up to the ranch house. Confused, she glanced at the clock. "They're home early."

Only, Travis soon discovered, the Cartwright women were not in the drive.

His parents were.

"I TAKE IT YOU WEREN'T expecting company?" Liz murmured, glancing out the window beside him. Nervously, she watched Kelsey and Brady Anderson emerge from the pickup truck bearing the Double Deal Ranch logo.

Travis's mother was as slim and fit as one would expect a woman rancher to be, her thick cinnamon-red hair, threaded with silver, falling over one shoulder in a loose braid. Brady was as tall and solidly built as his sons, and carried himself in the confident, purposeful manner of a wildly successful cattleman.

Neither looked happy at the moment.

Travis shook his head. "My folks must have heard about the suspension or the lawsuit—or both."

Liz finished gathering up the files. She knew how difficult a family confrontation could be. It was bad enough when it was your own. "Hey." She shot him a commiserating look. "If you want me to make myself scarce…"

Travis caught her arm and reeled her back. "No. You may as well be here. Before it's all over, they'll probably want to talk to you, too."

Short minutes later, after the four of them were settled in the ranch house living room, Travis asked, "How did you find out?"

"Grandpa Hargett. It's all over Houston," his father said tersely. "And with him still being CEO and owner of Anderson Oil...of course it's going to get back to him, that his grandson botched a big deal for another Houston oil company heiress."

"What was his reaction?"

"He wanted to know why in blazes we hadn't told him," Brady said. "Instead, he had to hear it at the Petroleum Club."

A muscle worked in Travis's jaw. "I'm sorry if he was embarrassed."

"He said he could get you another job, at the law firm that manages his personal affairs."

Reluctantly, Travis confessed, "I temporarily lost my license."

Watching, Liz hurt for him. This was any attorney's worst nightmare. And for one as gifted and ambitious as Travis...?

Brady Anderson waved that off. "Doesn't matter. Dad promised that they'd find something for you to do—and pay you a lot better than Haverty, Brockman & Roberts, too."

Kelsey sent her son a beseeching look. "I know how you feel about your independence. When I was your age, I felt the same way. But you really should let family help you. Your grandfather knows lawyers who have close ties to the upper reaches of the Texas legal community." She delicately cleared her throat. "Honey, all you have to do is talk to your grandfather...."

Travis knotted his fists. "No, Mom. I know you all mean well, but I'm not doing that." He stood, signaling that the family powwow was over. "I've got it handled."

"You know how I feel about nepotism and family influence," Brady said. "I've always wanted you kids to make your own way. But in this instance…" He and his wife exchanged looks. "We don't want to see you lose what you have worked so hard to achieve. And from what we understand, Olympia Herndon is a very vindictive woman, son. She doesn't take well to losing."

"Then she's going to have to learn," Travis vowed. He moved to show his parents to the door. "Now if you will excuse us, Liz and I really need to get back to working on my defense."

"Wow," she said when Travis returned, after seeing his parents off.

"See what I mean about interference?" he muttered.

Liz nodded, putting his dinner in the microwave to reheat. "Although it was well intentioned."

Travis shook his head. "My grandfather, Hargett Anderson, is even worse."

Liz carried Travis's plate to the table. "He's a very powerful man."

"Yes, he is." Travis waited while she reheated her own dinner. "Age hasn't slowed him down one bit."

Absently, Travis held Liz's chair for her, the way he would have if they'd been on a date.

Except, Liz cautioned herself sternly, this wasn't a date.

Calmly, she suggested, "It might not hurt to have Hargett make calls on your behalf. On the other hand…" she paused, as her next worry hit "…if the wrong thing is said, or something is misconstrued and people think he is trying to influence the state bar officials or the officers of the court where the malpractice suit will be heard…it could be seen as influence peddling."

His broad shoulders slumping, Travis ran a hand

through his hair. "Don't I know it. Which is why we have to move even faster," he stated urgently, looking Liz in the eye. "We've got to find a way to get this over and done with before my family gets more involved."

Liz understood the need to be independent.

She reached out to grip Travis's hand. "We'll talk to Digger Dobbs, find out what his take on the situation is, and go from there."

"You're taking a day off already?" Faye Elizabeth asked Travis in surprise, as they carried supplies in from the warehouse trip.

Liz hated parsing the truth, but in this case she had no choice—it was her client's wish. "I have to interview a roughneck on a drilling site a couple hours from here, for this employment case I'm working on. I'm not really sure what I'm walking into, so I asked Travis to go with me." Which was all true, Liz thought guiltily. As far as it went.

"By all means, take him," Reba exclaimed, setting down a twelve-pack of paper towels.

Liz flushed at her mother's double entendre, which, judging by the twinkle in her eye, was no accident.

Rolling her eyes at Reba's blatant matchmaking attempt, Tillie stopped organizing canned goods in the pantry long enough to pat her great-granddaughter on the arm. "That's very wise of you, dear. Those oil sites can be dangerous places. Better to be safe. And there's no wiser way to do that than by taking a big, strong, handsome hunk of a man with you."

Travis grinned, liking the description.

Liz snickered.

"Maybe you should ask an off-duty sheriff's deputy instead. Like Rio Vasquez or Kyle McCabe," Faye Elizabeth suggested, still obviously trying to think up ways to keep Liz and Travis apart.

Liz unloaded the contents of a cooler into the fridge. "I want Travis to come with me. And don't worry about anything here that we fall behind on," she said, before another protest could be made. "So you won't be left shorthanded, he's arranged for a cowboy from his parents' ranch to come by tomorrow in his stead, and help out until we get back."

"Which will be when?" Reba asked with a sly wink.

"Very late tomorrow evening." Liz just hoped—for both her and Travis's sake—that the result would be what they both wanted.

Liz and Travis met up at dawn. He drove. She used the time to prepare for the meeting with the key witness in the lawsuit against Travis.

Glad she had something to do other than gape at Travis and admire how handsome he was, Liz asked, "Explain to me why Olympia Herndon was so intent on buying out Digger Dobbs."

Suddenly looking as if he felt as uncomfortable sitting side by side with her in the cozy interior of his pickup truck, Travis held the wheel with one hand and reached for his sunglasses with the other. "He's one of the few experts in shale oil extraction who does not already work for a major petroleum company."

"And Herndon Oil does that?"

"They're trying to get an operation started," Travis explained with a beleaguered sigh. "But that requires substantial venture capital. Investors will chip in only if someone like Digger is on board to find and identify the reserves, and then oversee the extraction of the solidified oil from inside the rock. Which, as you can imagine, is a difficult, environmentally sensitive process."

"Olympia couldn't have gone to someone else?"

Travis stared out the windshield with a frown. "She wanted the best independent left, and that was Digger Dobbs."

Travis went on to explain why the wildcatter was the best.

After that, they talked about the billing, compensation and promotion practices of HB&R, as well as how Travis had excelled during his time at the firm. Until Olympia Herndon had wanted him fired.

Liz was ready to ask more about that, but time ran out.

"The drilling area is just around the next bend," Travis said.

She had never been to an underground extraction site. The in situ oil shale facility run by wildcatter Digger Dobbs resembled a maze of aboveground pipes and nodding donkeys, attached to reservoirs.

Trailers were parked around the perimeter, a distance away. A dozen dust-covered pickup trucks and vans filled a makeshift lot.

Travis nodded at a short, bowlegged man in grimy coveralls and a bright orange hard hat. Clipboard in hand, the deeply suntanned roughneck was reading what looked to be computer printouts. "Come on," Travis said gruffly, looking anything but eager to get this over with. "I'll introduce you."

They started in Digger's direction.

Before Liz or Travis could greet the boss of the operation, however, another car drove up. The doors to the sleek black SUV opened and three men and a woman got out.

Liz didn't have to ask who the leggy blonde in the trim white suit and heels was.

Olympia Herndon. In the flesh.

Digger glared at the other guests, then turned back and gave Travis an accusing look. "Your lawyer said she wouldn't be here."

"She's not supposed to be," Liz interjected.

Olympia strode forward, the three business-suited men flanking her. Ignoring Travis completely, she faced off with Liz. "You've got no business being here."

"Mr. Dobbs has consented to speak to us," Liz said.

"Actually, I'd prefer to speak to none of you," Digger grumbled. "But since you're all here, listen up and listen good. That young lawyer there—" he pointed to Travis "—did his damnedest to get me to sign with that pushy female." He pointed to Olympia. "What no one seems to understand is that it was never going to happen. I'm not selling out. I'm not joining any company. I'm my own boss and that's the way it is always going to be."

"And you'll swear to that in court?" Liz asked.

Opposing counsel grew even tenser as they realized their whole case was about to collapse.

Digger swore like a drunken sailor. "I'm sure as heck not going to lie! Now get the hell off my lease, all of you! You've worn out your welcome."

Olympia started to speak, then caught the gazes of her companions. She turned away from Digger, who was already striding off in a huff, and headed for Travis instead.

"I'll make a deal with you," his former client proposed, an avaricious gleam in her eyes. "Get your insurance company to settle my malpractice claim against you and I'll drop the lawsuit and the charges with the state bar, so you can get your law license back."

Some might have taken the deal just to get this over with, Liz noted. Not Travis. His jaw tensed. "I didn't do anything wrong."

Olympia shot him a coy look. "Really?" she purred. "Is that the way you want to play it?" she threatened silkily. "Because one way or another I'm going to recoup the money and the time I lost."

"How?" Liz asked.

The oil heiress had no case—or did she? Why— in the face of what they'd just learned—was opposing counsel still so confident? So willing to let their client take the lead?

An awkward silence fell.

"Think about it," Olympia advised, the threat in her voice unmistakable. "You have until tonight."

Pivoting, she glided off, her attorneys right behind her.

A few moments later, Liz and Travis headed for his pickup truck. She waited until they were cruising down the highway before she asked, "Mind telling me what that was about?"

Travis clenched his jaw. "You heard her. She wants to save face, and excoriating me is the way she has decided to do that."

Liz swiveled toward him. "It seems personal." Oddly so.

"Revenge always is," he said.

Travis's sunglasses shaded his eyes, and Liz wished she could rip off the dark lenses. Get closer. Do something, anything, to ferret out the truth. "For me to effectively represent you and bring this to closure I have to know everything," she pointed out.

Once again, Travis kept his eyes on the road. "I've told you everything pertinent to the case," he stated. Then why, Liz wondered, didn't she believe him?

Chapter Six

Liz and Travis got back to the ranch around eight that evening. He went straight to the barn to relieve the Double Deal cowboy they'd borrowed for the day. Liz headed inside, where all three Cartwright women awaited, clearly with romance on their mind.

"Did you get what you needed?" her mother asked, handing her a tall glass of lemonade.

The icy liquid eased Liz's thirst. "Yes and no." She wiped the corners of her lips with the back of her hand.

Eyebrows rose and everyone waited.

"It's clear my client is not guilty of the accusations against him, but the opposing forces seem to be increasing exponentially nevertheless."

Tillie sighed. "We have no idea what you're talking about."

"You're not supposed to." Liz plucked a blueberry muffin from a plate on the kitchen counter and started peeling off the wrapper. "It's a confidential client matter."

"I hope this doesn't mean you're going to get hopelessly involved with yet another underdog," Faye Elizabeth said, going over to the phone and returning with several sheets from the message pad, which she handed to her daughter. "The calls started coming in right after you left this morning."

"J.T. wants to know if you're going to be able to file his rezoning request with the town first thing tomorrow," Reba said. She flipped to the next page. "Hargett Anderson—Travis's grandfather—phoned, looking for him. He said, since he couldn't get Travis to call him back, maybe you could...?"

Reba struggled to read her own handwriting, which was as bad as Liz's. "And the last was from an attorney with Haverty, Brockman & Roberts—a Mr. Brockman. He was very nice. He said he hated to bother us on a Sunday 'cause he knew you'd recently taken on an important case, but he really needed to speak to you as soon as possible."

It was all Liz could do not to groan as she perused the messages her mom handed over.

Aware it wasn't Reba's fault, since they had purposefully kept everyone in the dark, she finished her muffin and walked over to toss the wrapper in the trash. "What did you tell him?"

"That you'd gone off to see some roughneck on a drilling site, west of Midland-Odessa. And we didn't know when you were going to be back."

"And he said...?" she prompted.

"He hoped you took someone with you, because it could be dangerous out there. And I told him," Reba continued indignantly, "that he didn't know the Cartwright women if he thought you couldn't take care of yourself. But that we had sent along our new ranch hand, Travis Anderson, just in case."

Well, that explained how the opposing counsel knew she and Travis were with Digger, Liz thought. And had gotten there just in time to thwart any headway they might have made.

"Have you eaten dinner?" Faye Elizabeth asked.

"Yes." Liz poured herself another glass of lemonade and drank deeply. "Travis and I got sandwiches at a restaurant on the road." Where he had spent most of the time deftly dodging her questions about the personal side of his relationship with Olympia Herndon.

She'd let it go, knowing it was going to take some finesse to get the information out of him. But he was going to have to spill all eventually, whether he liked it or not. Otherwise, she would not be able to properly represent him. Which, as a lawyer, he also knew.

Liz's cell phone vibrated. She pulled it out of her pocket and read the message coming across the screen. Once again, it was all she could do not to groan in dismay. "I'm going to have to go to the office."

"Tonight?" Tillie cried.

"Yes."

"But it's so late," she protested. "You shouldn't work so hard."

Liz hugged her great-grandmother and pressed a kiss on her fading red hair. "I'll ask Travis to go along with me."

"Are you sure there's no spark left between you?" Faye Elizabeth asked suspiciously.

"I hope there is!" Beaming, Tillie returned the hug, giving Liz an extra affectionate squeeze.

"Me, too," Reba said. "And that you keep your real goals firmly in mind."

Meaning having a baby and continuing the Cartwright family. Liz's goals, however, were far different from her mother's. She wanted to keep her life from becoming messy and emotional. Everything else was secondary.

"You don't need to worry about that, Mom," she told her.

Whatever Travis was keeping from her was reason enough to concentrate only on representing him.

Liz found him in the barn. He was tending to two calves that hadn't been thriving in the field, so had been stabled, along with their mamas, for a few days.

Hearing her approach, he emerged from the stall, a question in his slate-gray eyes.

"I just had an email from opposing counsel. They faxed an amended complaint to my office in town."

Travis looked as if he had been half expecting the perfectly legal—yet underhanded—tactics of his former law firm. "It can wait until tomorrow morning," he said with a grimace.

"Maybe for you," Liz countered. "I'm not going to lie awake all night wondering what is in it."

He exhaled, his frustration with the situation mounting. "In that case I'll go with you. Just give me a minute to wash up."

The ride to town was conducted in silence. Liz sensed Travis had an idea what was in the waiting fax. Her suspicion was confirmed the moment she got a look at the amended complaint.

Heart sinking, she handed the pages over. "Is this true?" she asked, half in shock, half in dismay.

The brooding look in his eyes intensified. "I had a relationship with Olympia," Travis admitted curtly.

Liz pushed aside the image of him and Olympia getting naked, and the hot flash of jealousy that followed. "A sexual relationship?"

"Yes."

"When she was your client?"

"Yes."

Hence the disclosure agreement he had presented Liz with the evening before. Suddenly, something that had seemed innocent—even thoughtful—at the time, took on a tawdry slant.

Resentment knotted her gut. A litany of not-so-nice words crowded her mind. "And you chose not to tell me?" Thereby leaving her in the dark, dammit!

"It wasn't relevant."

"I'm your attorney." Liz advanced on Travis, temper sizzling. She grabbed the papers from him and slammed them onto her desk, then whirled back to face him. "It's my job to decide what's relevant. It's your job to confide in me—not to keep things from me."

His eyes narrowed and a long pause followed. "Why are you so upset?" he asked.

Because once again Travis had been cutting her out, when he should have been including her.

Liz vowed to keep her emotional involvement with him to the absolute minimum from that moment on.

Swallowing, she walked around her desk, and sat down behind it. Clasped her hands together and said in a cool and professional tone, "I pride myself on doing the very best job I can to represent my clients."

She paused to let her words sink in.

Travis folded his big frame into one of the client chairs in front of her desk.

She continued with a censuring glare. "I was at a big disadvantage this afternoon because I was the only one there who didn't know what Olympia was threatening you with."

Travis shifted into a more comfortable position and propped one ankle on the opposite knee. He rubbed at a spot of distressed leather on his boot. "Not true." Slowly, deliberately, he lifted his eyes to hers. "Digger and the rest of his crew didn't know, either."

But all the attorneys had! His ex-lover slash client had! Liz gritted her teeth. "You really want to joke at a time like this?"

His pewter eyes grew shuttered. "There is nothing funny to me about this situation."

"You're right about that." Liz pushed her chair back and vaulted to her feet. She picked up the pages, shoving them into a file. "I should have known this would happen." She shook her head in anger. "You blindsided me before, breaking up with me when I least expected it. And now you have disrespected me again with your silence."

How the heck was she supposed to come back from that?

He rose, too, his expression sober. "This isn't a personal affront to you, Liz," he insisted in a low, sexy voice.

"The heck it isn't!" She rounded the desk and shoved the file into his hands.

"I made it clear to you when I first took your case. I can represent flawed clients, because everyone is entitled to a defense. But I won't represent clients who don't tell me the whole truth."

"You're firing me as a client?" The look on his face spoke volumes about what he thought of that.

"And as a ranch hand." Liz jerked her chin toward the door. "Good luck and Godspeed at finding your own way home." She paused to slay him with her eyes. "Because you and I, Travis?" she finished very softly. "We're done."

LIZ FIGURED TRAVIS WOULD have his belongings out of the homestead and off the Four Winds by the following morning, if not sooner.

Instead, she came down to breakfast Monday morning to find him sitting at the kitchen table, holding court over a sumptuous spread of eggs, bacon, sausage, hash brown potatoes, fruit and homemade biscuits with Faye Elizabeth's famous honey butter.

Noting that his appetite hadn't abated in the slightest, Liz skittered to a halt. "What are you doing here?"

Travis met her gaze, his eyes dark and heated.

The Cartwright women all looked at her as if she'd lost her mind. "He works here," Tillie reminded her.

Liz closed her eyes. When she opened them again, Travis was still looking at her. Daring her to say just about anything.

Liz frowned and turned to the ladies. "I fired him."

Reba shrugged. "Actually, you can only do that if you've taken over the reins of the Four Winds. And you haven't, so it's up to us. And we all want him to stay."

Muttering under her breath, Liz stomped over to the drying rack next to the sink, and rummaged around for her thermal coffee mug. All too aware of everyone's eyes on her, she moved to the coffeemaker and filled the mug two-thirds full.

Tillie handed her the toasted-coconut flavored creamer from the fridge, and gently brought her up to speed. "Travis told us he'd hired you to handle a legal problem for him, the two of you disagreed about how to proceed, and you quit. And then fired him. But—" Tillie patted Liz's arm "—we disagree with that."

Reba moved to Liz's other side. "We need his help. And Travis wants to stay. So…"

"…as long as the two of you are no longer attracted

to each other in that way," Faye Elizabeth said, "it makes sense for him to continue to work here."

Liz snapped the lid on her mug and set it on the counter with a thud. "Seriously." She marched over to Travis and stood facing him, hands on her hips. "Seriously?" she all but shouted, expecting him to stand and square off with her like a man.

Instead, he pushed his chair back from the table and made himself even more comfortable. Crinkles appeared at the corners of his gray eyes. "Just because you reneged on your half of our bargain doesn't mean I'm going to renege on mine."

It was all Liz could do not to grab him by the shirt and haul him to his feet.

Hanging on to her considerable temper by a thread, she said through gritted teeth, "I'd like a word with you, Travis Anderson." Before anyone else in the room could say anything, she snapped, "Alone!"

Tillie moved to Travis's side and patted him on the shoulder. "Better do as she says, dear," she encouraged kindly. "Our darling Liz doesn't get that fiery very often, but when she does it is best to hear her out."

Liz stormed outside. Aware they still had an audience, she kept right on going, all the way to the homestead. Jet and Mud were lying on the front porch, waiting for the day's work to begin. Despite herself, Liz could not pass a dog without pausing to pet it so she bent to quickly give each a scratch behind the ears, then continued on into the cabin.

She made it as far as the table, then spun around, pulse racing. "You must have better things to do than torment me."

"I can't think of any."

He was teasing her, but when she met his gaze he wasn't smiling.

Her stomach dropped. "Have you hired another lawyer?"

Something flickered in his expression at that. Annoyance at having to explain himself, probably. "Nope."

Liz huffed in frustration. "Tell me you're not going to represent yourself."

He stared at her. "I don't have plans to, no."

Liz had seen clients self-destruct before. It was never a pleasant experience.

"You have until three this afternoon to respond to their assertions," the advocate in her forced to point out. "Or they are going to file that amended lawsuit with the court."

He flexed his brawny shoulders, the motion as careless as his attitude. "Let 'em file."

"That's terrible legal strategy."

He stood, legs braced apart, arms folded in front of him. Showered but unshaved, and wearing a washed-'til-it-was-soft blue chambray shirt and faded jeans, Travis was every inch an indomitable Texan.

His gaze drifted over her, taking in her black sheath dress, pale pink cardigan and heels. Ever so slowly, he returned to her eyes. "Why do you care?"

Liz lifted her chin. "Because what is happening to you is an injustice."

He sent her a level look. "And injustice happens all the time."

"Not on my watch."

He came closer, appearing ready to show her the door. To what had until recently been her private domain!

Gently, he spun her around and directed her forward.

"As you pointed out," he said, his warm breath brushing her ear, "I'm not *on* your watch." He dropped his hand and moved back. "Not any longer."

Feeling as if she had been burned, Liz turned right back around. Determined to get through to him, for both their sakes, she spread her hands wide. "Look," she said in a much more cajoling voice, "sleeping with Olympia Herndon…sleeping with any client…was obviously a mistake." *Just like my taking on your case was.* But that didn't mean they couldn't remedy the situation.

Not that Travis looked in any way ready to cooperate with her, she realized in aggravation.

He lifted an eyebrow. "A mistake you would never make. Right?"

His sarcasm stung, even if it was on point.

Liz nodded, keeping her gaze level with his. "Right," she drawled, her voice every bit as goading as his had been.

Travis came closer, his expression like that of a lion stalking his prey. Slowly, deliberately, he grasped her elbows. "Sure about that?" he asked in a low, silky voice.

Liz swallowed, every inch of her going on white-hot alert. "Wh-what are you doing?" She stepped away, aware she was holding her breath.

He slowly danced her backward, toward the wall. "Putting your willpower and integrity to the test."

The feel of his tall, muscular frame pressed up against her trembling body sent a shimmer of need sifting through her. "Travis…"

He brushed his thumb along her jaw, then her lips, the soft pressure encouraging them to part. "I'm not your client anymore, Liz." He touched his mouth to hers, all too briefly. "I'm not even your friend."

He bent his head and kissed her again, his lips tenderly coaxing and recklessly taking, his sensual mouth moving over hers, until she wreathed her arms about his neck and kissed him back every bit as passionately as he was kissing her.

When he finally lifted his head, she asked breathlessly, "What is your point?"

"That I'm human," he told her gruffly, tracing the contours of her face and looking deep into her eyes. "And so are you." Travis kissed her again, letting all the emotion he'd been holding back flow into the potent embrace.

Liz had always wondered what it would have been like if she and Travis had started dating when they were a lot older. When sex was more a way to connect with someone than a forbidden mystery.

Now she knew.

"We're going to regret this," she murmured, even as she savored the sensations he sent spiraling through her body.

"I know." He wrapped his arms around her and brought her flush against him. Brushing her hair aside, he kissed his way down her throat.

Liz reveled in the feel of him, so hard and hot and masculine. She turned her lips back to his. "It'll never happen again."

He chuckled, already guiding her toward the bed. "I know you think that," he murmured. And then their kisses intensified, until he was all she felt, all she knew, and there was no denying she wanted this. Wanted him. With all her heart and soul.

For the first time in her life, she let herself go, let the heat slash through her. The only sound in the room was their heavy breathing as they undressed each other and tumbled onto the bed.

Liz writhed beneath his touch, her own fingers finding the hard, sensitive places on his body. They rolled again and then he was dropping lower, until he was at the apex of her thighs. She gasped and caught his head, shuddering helplessly and gasping for air. But there was no rushing him, not even when he paused to find a condom and roll it on. Not when he lingered over her breasts and slid between her thighs.

He took her where she wanted to go with seemingly no effort at all, diving deep. The sensations filled her with an intense driving need, and they surged together in sweet, perfect unison until she lost track of everything but the need to surrender to the blinding pleasure of the moment.

Afterward, they lay together, quiet…breathless. And that was when Liz's cell phone rang.

Happy for the distraction—anything to keep her from thinking too hard or too long about what she had just done—she reached for her BlackBerry. Noted the caller ID. Sighed.

Draping the sheet around her, she moved from the bed. Clicked on. "J.T. Good morning to you, too. No, I haven't submitted anything to the city yet. And I'm not going to until after I talk to the pool company and the surveyor and the town engineer about possible solutions to your problem." She rubbed her temples as J.T. prattled on. "Maybe not, but it never hurts to try to forge a solution that satisfies everyone before heading to court. I understand. Give me until Thursday to see what I can work out, and we'll meet in my office. Um… four o'clock okay with you? All right. See you then."

Liz touched the screen with her fingertip and ended the call.

Feeling a little more in control, now that she was back to business, she glanced over her shoulder at Travis, who was still lounging in the bed. Looking incredibly satisfied and content.

"This was a mistake."

Now that she had her wits about her, she couldn't believe she had allowed him to make love with her to prove a point. And that she was so susceptible to his hot, passionate advances.

Travis exhaled roughly and sat up. "You said that already."

Liz snatched up her clothes and went into the bathroom to dress.

When she came out, she picked up where they had left off. "We're like oil and water."

Travis snapped the buttons on his shirt. Tucked it into his jeans. "I thought we mixed pretty well just now."

She slid her feet into her heels. "Don't joke." *Not about my vulnerability, or yours—and certainly not about the loneliness that drove us to do this....*

Because if either of them was in love with anyone else, this would not have happened.

Travis sobered and silence stretched between them.

Liz knew if she wasn't careful she would fall all the way in love with him. "I want you to hire someone else to represent you."

Travis shook his head, his jaw rigid. "There's no point. It's a 'he said, she said' situation. I don't want my family name dragged through the muck."

Liz stared at him in frustration. "You have Dobbs willing to testify on your behalf."

Travis shrugged off the coup. "I know my former bosses. They'll muddy the waters as much as they feel necessary to succeed in winning this lawsuit for Olympia, and keeping the Herndon Oil business in-house."

He shoved his fingers through his hair. "If she hadn't gone public with the affair, who knows what might have happened…but it's clear now she'll stop at nothing to trash my name and reputation. And there is a point," he concluded grimly, "where it's just not worth it."

Liz shook her head in admonishment. "You'd give up the law?" she asked incredulously. "Because that's what is at stake here, Travis—your license to practice."

He was silent a beat too long. "There are times when it's more important to keep your dignity and self-respect than cling to some hard-won goal." His words were short and clipped. "This is one of them."

"I HAVE A BETTER IDEA," Liz declared.

Travis lifted his head, unable to match her resolve. "Yeah? And what's that?"

His mood grim, he located his boots and sat down on the edge of the bed.

Vibrating with energy, Liz came closer, watching as he shoved his feet into them.

Finished, Travis looked up at her, resting a forearm on his knee. Hard to believe he had just made love to her—this feisty, beautiful woman he'd never suspected would let herself go.

But she had opened up the floodgates of desire. And he couldn't get over it.

The Liz he had known before had backed off after a few kisses, too much of a kid to enjoy them. The grown-up Liz clearly reveled in kisses.

Had the circumstances been different, he'd have her

back in his bed right now, proving his desire for her, all over again. Just to make sure she knew it was as genuine as his growing attraction to her.

But that wasn't going to happen.

Not this morning, anyway.

Not with chores and cattle waiting, and the world outside already crowding in.

Liz offered a hand, pulling him to his feet. "Let's fight 'em with all our might."

Travis rubbed his jaw, considering. "I thought you'd quit."

She finger combed her hair restoring order. "I've decided I want back in."

He found her a brush. "As my lawyer or my lover?"

"Lawyer." She walked to the mirror to repair the damage the roll in the sack had done, and she caught his eyes in the glass. "The lover business still has to go."

Travis came up behind her, with effort keeping his hands to himself. Quietly, he challenged, "Suppose I'd rather have the latter?"

Liz turned and slapped the brush back in his palm. She glided past him in a drift of lavender perfume, being careful not to touch him. "You're not thinking clearly right now, so I'm going to forget you said that." She paused a safe distance away, then stated, "What I would like you to do is this—authorize me to contact HB&R on your behalf, and tell them we are prepared to not only deny all charges but file a countersuit for unlawful termination against Haverty, Brockman & Roberts. Plus a defamation suit against Olympia Herndon."

Travis studied her, admiring her never-ever-give-up attitude. "And you think this will get us…?"

"For starters? A much better bargaining position. And a delay in anything being filed. That will give us time to do a little sleuthing and strategizing on our own, as well as prepare for the deposition they are likely to insist upon, before all is said and done."

"I've already told you everything that's relevant."

"I doubt it," Liz replied airily, making sure her appearance was intact before she headed out the door. "But before we're done—" she paused to glance deep into Travis's eyes "—I promise that you will."

Chapter Seven

Determined to get a quick and easy solution for at least one of her clients, Liz looked at the men sitting around the conference table in her office. "The three of you have the power to fix this problem," she told them sternly.

Steve Wylin, from Custom Pools, threw up his hands. "I already designed what J.T. wanted."

Liz held Steve's gaze. "You know the town is never going to allow him to have a swimming pool in his front yard."

Clyde Burns, the town planner, turned to Liz. "Which is why you should convince J.T. to table the whole thing."

"I agree with that," J.T.'s neighbor, Tim Patrone, said, looking as irritated as ever. "Furthermore, why isn't J.T. here?"

"Because he is too emotional right now to be in on this conversation." Liz frowned. "And the three of you should show some compassion." She leaned forward earnestly. "Imagine you had lost the love of your life, your constant companion for the last forty years. You'd be grief-stricken and overemotional, too."

"I don't see it as our problem," Clyde argued.

"Well, it's not. Except..." Liz deliberately made eye

contact with all three men "…if you don't work together to find a solution, the three of you will likely be embroiled in a lengthy battle." She paused to let her warning sink in. "'Cause I know J.T. He is not going to give up on this idea."

Silence fell.

"On the other hand," she continued, more gently now, "if the three of you put your heads together and figure out a solution that captures the essence of what J.T. is trying to do, and would be acceptable to the neighborhood, then I am sure I can convince him to scale back his expectations and accept your proposal in the spirit that it is given."

The men exhaled and exchanged looks.

"It can't hurt to try," Clyde said finally.

"Deep down, he is a good guy," Tim added. "Just eccentric."

"And I would still like to sell a pool," Steve admitted.

This, they all knew, was the only way it would happen.

"So we're in agreement?" Liz asked, standing.

The men nodded. Handshakes sealed the deal.

Liz was in the process of showing them all out when the door opened and Travis walked in.

Though she had promised herself she would be immune to him emotionally from here on out, her heart skipped a beat at the sight of him.

He was still wearing the ranch clothes he'd had on that morning, only now the chambray shirt and denim jeans were covered with smudges of dirt and grass stains, and the stubble on his handsome jaw looked even silkier. It gave him a ruggedly sexy appeal.

Telling herself to ignore her reaction, she said, "Everything okay?"

He nodded, his attention on ranch matters once again. "We've got fifty calves that are now a month old. They need their first set of vaccinations, and your mom wants it done this evening."

Uh-oh. "It's a two-person job, even after you get them separated from their mamas," Liz said.

He nodded. "I offered to bring in an extra hand, but Reba refused to hear of it. She said that tradition requires a Cartwright woman be part of the inoculating team."

Liz sensed a matchmaking scheme kicking into high gear. "Let me guess... Mom volunteered me over Faye Elizabeth's protests." Without bothering to check Liz's schedule. So what was new?

Travis gave her a look that said *I wish*. He shook his head. "*She's* going to do it."

Liz groaned. "And likely reaggravate her sciatica in the process."

"I agree it's a bad idea." Travis hissed out a breath and shrugged. "But Reba's running the ranch...."

Liz came closer, inhaling the man-leather-and-horse scent of him. She stared at his broad shoulders. Shoulders that right now were carrying too much. "So Mom gets to make all the decisions."

Travis acknowledged that with a slight bow of his head. "You could change that. All you'd have to do is take over the reins, like your family wants...."

Liz drew a shaky breath and gave up trying to explain her resistance to being put in charge. She had too much responsibility on her own shoulders right now. "It's not that simple and you know it."

His eyes filled with understanding, and he touched

her cheek. "I do." Emotional connection made, he dropped his hand, stepped back. "But I'm also not in a position to tell your mother what to do. My job—at the moment, anyway—is to follow orders. And right now I'm on my way over to the vet's office to pick up the vaccines that Reba ordered this morning."

Tingling from the brief, tender contact, Liz beckoned him toward her private office. "Aren't you going to ask about your case?"

He fell into step behind her. "I figured if there was anything to report, you'd tell me."

Liz sighed. "I faxed the letter threatening counterlitigation this morning, and I gave them until five o'clock to respond."

Travis grinned, appreciating the legal gamesmanship. "Which means they'll send something at 4:57."

"Probably." Liz answered his cryptic smile with one of her own. "In the meantime…tell Mom not to sweat it, that I'll help you with the inoculations this evening."

Travis frowned, looking as reluctant to overburden her as she was to overwork him. "Sure about that?" he drawled.

Trying not to get too excited about the evening— it would be hard work, after all, and lots of it—Liz nodded. "Absolutely. By then, the initial response of opposing counsel should be in." For a moment, she indulged in a romantic whim and let her gaze linger on the rugged contours of his face. "We can talk about what our next step should be while we work."

Liz PHONED HER MOTHER as soon as Travis left, and told her she'd be coming back to the ranch shortly. "But there is something I want from you in return…."

"You're sure J.T. wants company tonight?" Reba asked.

"It doesn't matter, Mom. He needs it. And if you want me at the ranch, you're going to have to help me keep him out of trouble."

Her mother chuckled. "Doesn't sound like I have any choice. I'll get right on it."

An hour and a half later, Liz drove up to the ranch house.

Her grandmother's sedan was parked in front of the house, its trunk open. Tillie was loading cleaning supplies, a vacuum cleaner and a mop. Faye Elizabeth was putting in a cooler and two insulated food carriers for hot dishes.

Liz moved quickly to lend a hand. "What's going on?"

Tillie frowned. "Have you been in J. T. Haskell's home recently?"

"No." Liz tensed, leery of receiving any more bad news. "Why?"

Faye Elizabeth leaned close. "Reba called from town. Apparently, it's a complete disaster. The fridge is empty except for cookies and beer. No wonder the man's a mess. Apparently, he hasn't had a decent meal since he can't remember when."

Tillie got in the passenger seat. "The man needs help and we're going to give it to him. And we'd do it even if we didn't owe him."

Liz knew that was true. Life in Laramie County was all about neighbor helping neighbor. Still… "Did J.T. agree to that?"

Tillie grinned. "From what I heard, your mother didn't give him much choice. Besides, what man in his right mind turns down Faye Elizabeth's home cooking?"

Good point, Liz thought. "How long are you going to be gone?" *And how long will Travis and I be alone out here?*

"Don't know." Her grandmother shrugged. "We'll call."

Liz could see Travis working in the pasture closest to the barn. As always, he was a sight to behold—the picture of raw capability and masculine efficiency. And it looked as if he had his hands full at the moment.

The cows were on one side of the fence, their calves already in the corral. Moos of displeasure echoed across the countryside.

While the ladies drove off, Liz hurried inside the ranch house to change.

By the time she got out to the corral where the chute was located, the frantic mooing and calling of cows and calves had escalated.

Travis glanced up at her. "Ready to get started?"

Trying not to think what it would be like to have him here on a permanent basis, Liz nodded.

If she was going to keep from falling into bed with him again, she was definitely going to have to burn off some emotional energy.

She pulled on her leather work gloves. "Let's get to it."

Together, they headed toward the pasture.

Around sixty-five pounds at birth, the calves now weighed about a hundred and ten. They were used to being handled gently, as all the Four Winds cattle were, so showed little fear as Travis approached them one by one and maneuvered them onto their side. He held them firmly while Liz administered the five inoculations, starting with IBR/P13 into each nostril. The vaccinations for haemophilus, pasteurella, leptospirosis and clostridial disease were given intramuscularly.

When she'd finished, they let the calf up and turned it into another corral, with troughs of water and creep feed.

Then on to the next.

Forty-nine more times, they administered protection and turned the baby calves out to feed. All the while, their mothers mooed and paced and watched protectively from the other side of the fence.

Finally, it was all done.

Liz opened the corral gates, and Travis shooed the calves through. Mamas and babies were reunited in the adjacent pasture, and suddenly the ranch was serenely quiet once again.

Liz turned to him. Though filthy, sweaty and smelling of cows, she had never been happier.

He looked pretty satisfied, too, and gazed at her in gratitude. "How about we both get cleaned up and meet at the ranch house?"

He hadn't so much as touched her, yet his glance warmed her through and through.

Liz smiled. "Sounds good to me," she said.

FORTY-FIVE MINUTES LATER, Liz cradled the phone to her ear. "What do you mean, you're not coming home 'til midnight?" she demanded of her mother, waving Travis into the Four Winds kitchen with her free hand.

Reba shouted to be heard above the voices in the background. "The evening is young and we've decided to teach J.T. to play SKIP-BO." There was a chorus of laughter. "Can you believe he's never learned?"

Liz knew the card game was incredibly popular with

senior citizens in Laramie, far surpassing the old stand-bys of bridge and poker. "It sounds like fun, Mom. You all be careful driving home."

Reba chuckled flirtatiously and murmured something to J.T. that Liz couldn't quite catch. "Oh, for heaven's sake, honey. You don't need to worry about that. Of course we will. And don't wait up." She ended the call.

Travis came closer.

Darkness had fallen outside, but the kitchen lights cast a cozy golden glow, making the room feel close and intimate.

A sensation made more so by the tall, rugged man smelling of soap.

He sauntered closer, his eyes filled with the easy affection he showed to all his friends. "Everything okay?"

Telling herself that was all they would be—friends—Liz took the lid off the Crock-Pot. The mouthwatering aroma of a hearty beef stew filled the room.

Ignoring the pebbling of her nipples against her bra, she bent to look in the silverware drawer. "Seems to be. The ladies are staying in town to play cards with J.T., so they won't be home until later."

Accepting her wordless offer to help himself to the food on the counter, Travis filled his plate. "You're surprised."

Liz took butter and jam out of the fridge, along with a pitcher of mint-flavored iced tea, and set them on the table next to the cloth-covered basket of sourdough biscuits. "It sounded like J.T. was actually having fun."

"Three Cartwright women plying him with good food and better company? What's not to like? And yet... you don't trust it."

Liz sat down opposite Travis. She spread her napkin on her lap, glad she had someone other than family to confide in. "I'm happy J.T. is getting some respite from his grief."

Travis forked up a tender carrot dripping in gravy. "But you don't think it will last, do you."

Reluctantly, Liz admitted, "No. Unfortunately, I don't." She took a bite and found the stew to be as melt-in-your-mouth delicious as it smelled. "But I'll take the reprieve."

"Speaking of difficult situations…"

They had planned to talk while they worked, but it had proved impossible. At times during the inoculations the noise had been damn near deafening.

Liz took a deep breath, sat back in her chair and forced herself into lawyer mode. "The only thing I got was an email at the end of the day, telling me that opposing counsel plan to talk with Olympia. Everything is on hold until she has a chance to weigh in, and they don't expect that to be until late Friday, at the earliest."

Travis's brows lowered angrily. "They're stalling and strategizing. Their next move will probably be to call a face-to-face meeting."

"Unless they decide to sue anyway and go straight to depositions. In either case," Liz promised, reassuring Travis with a frank look, "I plan to be ready for whatever they throw at us next." She forked up more stew with gusto. "Which means you and I have a lot of prep work to do, too."

Travis drummed his fingers on the table. "Such as…?"

Liz tried not to think about what those same hands had done to her earlier in the day. "I need background information," she said bluntly. "Everything and anything opposing counsel might ask you about."

THE LAST THING TRAVIS wanted to talk to Liz about was the trouble that had ended his employment with Haverty, Brockman & Roberts.

"We've already put in two very full days." He stood and carried his plate to the sink. "Can't this wait until tomorrow?"

"I guess that depends." She tilted her head, considering. "Just how badly do you want your law license reinstated?"

Travis put his dishes in the dishwasher. "A week ago, I would have said it was the most important thing on earth to me." He went back to finish clearing the table.

"And now?" she asked softly.

"I keep asking myself if it's going to be worth it to have my dirty laundry dragged out for everyone to see." He braced a hip against the counter. "There are other ways I can use my education."

Liz pressed her lips together. "That would be a terrible shame, because you are one fine lawyer."

The conviction in her voice surprised him. "How do you know?" he challenged.

She looked at him in a way that made all rational thinking cease. "I looked up some of your cases last night, read some of your briefs," she admitted. "Pretty amazing stuff for an associate."

You're pretty amazing. Shrugging, he explained the reason for his expertise in a field many attorneys found daunting. "I spent time with my grandpa Anderson, both in the oil patch and at Anderson Oil refineries, when I was a kid. He made sure that I understood how important it was to know the industry if I wanted to be a successful oil and gas attorney."

"Is that why Olympia Herndon wanted you to represent her?" Liz asked curiously, reaching for the coffee. "Because of your background?"

Travis fitted a paper filter into the plastic funnel and snapped it into the machine. He stepped back to give Liz room. "She knew my grandfather was Hargett Anderson."

Liz opened the can and spooned coffee into the filter. "And I'm guessing so did the law firm that hired you."

The fragrance of French roast coffee rose up between them. Travis nodded in answer to her question, adding, "HB&R wanted me to bring Anderson Oil business into the firm, but my grandfather has his own in-house legal team."

Liz's lower lip twisted pensively. "Did you give them any illusions about what your family connections might yield, in terms of clients? Or in any way infer that you could convince Hargett to jettison his in-house team and go with you and HB&R?"

"No." Travis added the proper amount of water to the coffeemaker and stood back as Liz switched it on. "I made it clear that was not going to be the case, that even if it was offered I would not accept any nepotism."

Liz rummaged around in the fridge, finally emerging with the remains of a pecan pie and a can of whipped cream. She got down a couple plates. "Did they believe you?"

Travis reached for the silverware. "In the final analysis? Probably not. Which is why I had to go all-out to land other big clients, without drawing on the accomplishments of other family members."

Liz cut two generous slices and put them on the plates. "And were you successful at that?"

"I was getting there." Travis watched as she shook the can and squirted swirls of cream onto each piece.

He caught her hand in his, scooped off a glob of cream and lifted it to her mouth. "And I thought we weren't going to talk business tonight."

"You said that." She caught her breath as he smeared whipped cream across her lower lip. "I never agreed."

Travis thought about what she would look like covered with the decadent topping. He caught her by the waist and tugged her against him. Lowered his head. "Maybe it's time you did."

With a hint of mischief glimmering in her green eyes, Liz licked the cream off her lip.

He grinned, nodding toward the aerosol can. "There's plenty more where that came from."

She flushed, her nipples pressing against her shirt. "This is a bad idea," she told him with a moan. But she didn't move away.

Travis took that as an invitation. He caught her chin in his hand, threaded his other through her hair. "I've been thinking about it all day," he murmured. "Wishing I could turn back the clock. Wishing we had never broken up. Wishing I could kiss you, just one more time."

So he did.

Chapter Eight

Travis had often wondered, in retrospect, if the emotional punch of his teenage romance with Liz had been exaggerated.

He found his memories did not do Liz justice. Making out with her was an amazing experience.

Everywhere he touched her she was strong and warm and feminine. Her kisses were evocative and intimate, but there was eroticism to the passion now, a woman's knowledge and desire that had not been there before.

This was no wary virgin he was kissing now, but an adult who had survived life's disappointments and triumphed over every professional challenge, with her confidence about the future intact.

Damned if her enthusiasm wasn't catching....

As RIBBONS OF DESIRE unfurled inside her, a wave of longing swept through Liz. She curled into Travis's embrace and deepened their kiss, her limbs heavy and weak, her skin tingling.

She'd never felt like this. Never felt as wanted as she did when she was in Travis's arms. She'd never had the lusty, physical side of her take control, or dreamed that the two of them might actually get another chance.

Unable to help herself, she ran her fingers through

his hair and rose up on tiptoe. Pressed her breasts against the muscles of his chest, and heard him groan. Damn, but she'd missed him.

He grasped her closer still and plundered her mouth, dominating and persuasive.

Liz clutched his shoulders, wanting nothing more than to go to bed with him. But she couldn't go forward without looking back in time first. She couldn't be that reckless again. Not without getting hurt.

She moaned, this time in protest, and pushed him away.

As much as she wanted him—and she did—she couldn't let herself be sucked back into the emotional whirlwind of a tryst with him unless she knew what had really happened years ago. And whether it would happen again.

Breathlessly, she stepped back and forced herself to stare into his charcoal-gray eyes. "I want the truth, Travis," she said. "Why did you really break up with me?"

Travis looked surprised, as if that was the last thing he'd imagined her asking. She absorbed his deepening frown.

"I know what you said at the time," Liz continued, wishing she hadn't blurted out the question that had nagged at her forever, or let herself be so vulnerable again.

She swallowed and pushed on. "That I was still in high school and you were going off to college. Our age difference was too great. We weren't what each other needed."

But you were what I wanted—and needed, she thought plaintively.

Travis stepped into her space. "There was also the

fact we were both so busy we hardly ever saw each other."

His goals again.

And hers.

"Would it have made a difference if I had been more open to...you know..."

"Climbing into the back of a car with me?"

Liz flushed.

"I was eighteen. My hormones were raging. But..." he sighed "...I was also smart enough to know that in that regard we were definitely not in the same place."

"So you left."

"Because we were way too young to be thinking about getting serious." His smile came, sure and slow. "And sleeping with you then, Liz, even working up to it, however incrementally, would have meant getting very serious."

And that, she thought, would have meant they would have indulged in a lot more than simply kissing good-night at the end of their dates.

All of a sudden the kitchen felt hot and close.

Liz ducked out the back door, into the spring night. The cool April air was damp and scented with the smells of fresh cut grass, and the flowers her great-grandmother had planted in the half barrels next to the house.

Liz stared out at the pasture and the clouds moving rapidly overhead.

It was going to rain. She could feel it in the air, and the cattle knew it, too. The cows were already nudging their calves toward the sheltering trees along the fence.

Liz folded her arms in front of her and held her chin high when Travis joined her. "I admit I wasn't ready for more…." *Wasn't ready to completely risk my heart. Not then. Not now.*

He grasped her hips and pulled her close, and she swallowed. "So when you sat me down to have that talk, and broke up with me, I just accepted it as the logical thing to do—even though my gut told me there was more to your decision than what you said. But now…" she dropped her forehead to his chest "…I really need to understand."

Travis ran one hand up and down her spine. Sifted the other through her hair. He pressed his forehead to hers, reached for her hand and gave it a squeeze. "When we first got together, I thought we were the same. Part of it was because of your family. Cartwright women are notorious for not wanting or needing a relationship with a man to be happy."

Liz tilted her head to one side. "Andersons are just as independent."

He grinned, not about to argue. "The rest had to deal with the fact that we both were very ambitious." He let her go and stepped back. "We both wanted to be lawyers. We both worked hard in school and on our ranches." His lips compressed in a wry, self-effacing smile.

"I thought we'd be able to date casually and have a good time and that when it came time for me to go off to college, you and I would part as friends."

"And yet when it actually came time for you to leave…"

He flashed a wry smile. "I realized it wasn't that simple."

Liz waited, sensing there was more.

Travis exhaled sharply. "Because of my relationship with you, I was losing focus." He paused, his expression matter-of-fact. "I knew that if we were going to achieve our dreams, we needed to finish growing up and to pursue our goals with the single-minded dedication we were both known for."

"So you have no regrets," Liz ascertained, not surprised, but disappointed nevertheless.

Because *she* had regrets. About all the things she hadn't said. Or done...

Travis slowly, patiently closed the distance between them once more. "About what I did then? No. No regrets." His gaze ardently traced her face, lingering on each feature in turn. He rubbed his thumb across her lip, absorbing the dewy moisture from their kiss. "It was the right decision for both of us at that time." His expression gentled. "But now—now is a different situation entirely."

Liz knew she should keep her distance.

Travis had crushed her dreams once and would surely do so again, when they found themselves in a different place. But as he pulled her against him, lowered his head and kissed her deeply, her will to fight faded as quickly as it had appeared.

Being with him like this felt like the most natural thing in the world. It felt right. So right, that with a little bit of luck, and more maturity... She opened her mouth to his, stroking his tongue with hers. With unrestrained passion, she surged against him, tempted by his warmth and his strength.

Travis responded, seeming to promise that if she dared give them another chance, the second time around would be so much sweeter and more fulfilling....

And that was when the sound of car engines came to their awareness and a blinding beam of light swept over them.

Embarrassed to be caught in a clinch, Liz broke off the impetuous kiss and stepped back. She lifted her arm to shield her eyes.

Silence reigned once again as the motors were cut, the headlamps faded.

Tillie and Faye Elizabeth got out of the sedan. Reba climbed down from the Four Winds Ranch pickup.

Hoping to divert their attention, and feel less like a reckless teenager caught in a heated clinch, Liz stepped forward. "What are you doing home so early?" Ignoring the tingling of her lips, she pretended a nonchalance she couldn't begin to feel. "I thought you were staying late, to play cards."

Tillie sighed. "Reba asked about an afghan crocheted by J.T.'s late wife, and that was all it took to get him upset. He asked us to leave, so we did."

Liz winced. "I'm sorry to hear that."

"J.T. wants you to call him first thing, for an update about his rezoning request," her mother added.

No doubt he would be as irascible as ever, too. "I'll take care of it," she promised as the first spattering of raindrops landed on her head.

Faye Elizabeth put up a hand to shield her hair, and headed for the door. "Coming in?" she asked Liz.

The invitation was clearly not extended to Travis.

"In a minute," she promised.

Over her shoulder, her grandmother warned, "Don't stay out here too long. We don't want you getting soaked to the skin."

Tillie followed her daughter. "Travis is such a gentleman. I am sure he won't let that happen."

"As long as something does," Reba teased.

The three elder Cartwrights disappeared inside the house.

Chagrined, Liz turned to Travis.

The two of them ducked beneath the roof of the back porch. "Sorry about that." She flushed.

Travis turned to face her and propped one shoulder against the limestone ranch house. "Score two for us resuming a relationship," he remarked.

Was that what he thought it was? Liz wondered, both excited by the notion and distressed by the arrogance of the assumption.

Rain fell in fat drops, splattering on the grass and scenting the air.

"One against," Travis continued.

Sadly, there was no saving either of them from Faye Elizabeth's disapproval.

"That pretty much sums it up." Liz sighed.

"The real question is—" Travis drew her close enough to feel his body heat "—what do *you* want?"

Liz knew she didn't want a fling. Marriage—or even the hope of anything permanent and long-lasting— scared her, since love never worked out for Cartwright women. The odds of finding any middle ground were just as poor.

To spare them both further discomfort and embarrassment, she concentrated on what they could easily discuss. "I want the Four Winds Ranch to thrive again." Liz paused to take a deep, enervating breath. "So I'd prefer the two of us to concentrate on accomplishing that."

"THANK HEAVENS it finally stopped raining," Reba remarked when Travis walked into the ranch house kitchen the next morning.

"An inch or two at a time is good," he said.

"Much more than that and we start having problems with all sorts of things, like flooding," she stated.

Fortunately, the creeks and rivers weren't high enough to make that a problem anytime soon, Travis thought.

"And debris-clogged creek beds." Reba motioned for him to have a seat at the table, treating him like the "family" she hoped he would become. At least long enough to give her a grandbaby. "Speaking of over-growth…we have to do something soon about the way the cedar and scrub are taking over the southern part of the ranch."

"I agree," Travis said as Liz walked in, dressed in an indigo business suit and ivory shell. With a leather business carryall looped over her shoulder, and her red hair drawn back in a knot at the nape of her neck, she looked elegant—and aloof. And he wanted nothing more than to get her horizontal again.…

"Morning, all," she said briskly, oblivious to the sensual nature of his thoughts.

Travis knew the way the previous evening ended had been his fault. In trying to make up for lost time and opportunity, he had pushed her too fast, too hard. Not surprisingly, she had become overwhelmed and put on the brakes. It was up to him to start over, and this time proceed at a pace she could accept. Would she give him a chance?

Liz took her travel mug off the rack.

Faye Elizabeth frowned in concern. "Please tell me you're going to take the time to have breakfast."

Liz's spine stiffened defensively. A hint of pink stole into her cheeks, making her look even prettier.

"I wish I could, but I really need to get to the office."

"Nonsense." Reba narrowed her eyes, declaring,

"You can stay for five minutes and talk ranch business with us."

Tillie smiled and, trying a softer approach, handed Liz one of her famous, freshly baked triple-chocolate scones. "Breakfast is the most important meal of the day."

Liz gave her great-grandmother a look. Everyone there knew pastries were one of her weaknesses.

"Five minutes," she said, reluctantly sitting in the only vacant chair, the one directly opposite Travis.

Appreciating the view, but also concerned for Liz's well-being, and not about to delay her unnecessarily, Travis said, "Back to the scrub and cedar overtaking the southern part of the ranch. I'd be happy to start clearing that for you."

Reba hunted for the bottle of ibuprofen and shook some into her hand. "I'm looking at a more long-term solution to the problem."

Liz tensed, as if she knew what was coming next.

Her mother swallowed a couple of pills and continued, "You can run about five goats per acre, and they'll keep it clear of brush. All you have to do is supplement them with feed and move them around, from one rocky, overgrown patch to another."

Travis suddenly understood why Liz was unhappy. The women couldn't handle the livestock they had. To bring on more, for whatever reason, would only add to the burden.

Tillie handed Travis a bowl of fresh strawberries and blueberries. "Your folks don't have any goats, do they?"

"No, ma'am." Wondering if there was anything he could do to help Liz without overstepping his bounds, he helped himself to a generous serving of the succulent fruit. "They've got their hands full with my mom's horses and my dad's cattle."

Faye Elizabeth passed the platter of scrambled eggs and breakfast sausages. "They also have half a dozen cowboys in their employ, to run their tractors."

"If you want, I could see about borrowing equipment and a few hands from my parents, to help us get caught up," Travis offered.

Insulted, Faye Elizabeth countered stiffly, "We're not asking for charity."

Liz picked up her empty plate and pushed back her chair. "I think the concern is how we're going to get by when you leave."

Ouch. Travis looked at Liz.

"We have to come up with a system that works with what resources we have now, and are liable to still have when the time comes and you move on."

Ouch again, Travis thought, noting Liz would not meet his eyes. Although he supposed she'd made a fair point.

Once his suspension was lifted, he would not be the chief hired hand here. And he had the sense they would not have the funds to hire much of a replacement, if any.

"What's your opinion on the subject?" he asked Liz, taking his plate to the sink, too. "Goats or no goats?"

She moved several inches to the left, to keep their bodies from touching, and continued avoiding his eyes.

So she was upset about the possibility—make that probability—of his leaving.

Oddly enough, Travis realized, he felt a little dejected about it, too. Although why...

It wasn't as if they would never see each other.

There was no way he was allowing them to lose contact again.

Liz inhaled and moved away from the sink. "Whether or not the ranch gets goats isn't for me to say."

"Of course it is!" the other three Cartwright women said in unison, heartily encouraging her. "You're part of the Four Winds Ranch, too."

"I'm not disputing my heritage," Liz retorted, looking a little pale and a lot exhausted.

In the sunlight streaming through the windows, Travis could see stress tightening the corners of her lips, and disillusionment in her eyes.

There was too much pressure on her.

She picked up her bag and slung it over her shoulder. "I have no thoughts on the matter," Liz stated mildly.

Sidestepping an argument was not the way to handle the women in her family. Avoiding the conflict would just make it harder for her later on.

Travis leaned back against the counter, hands braced on either side of him, and deliberately took Liz on. "I don't believe that," he drawled, and saw her brow arch.

He met her gaze and continued, "You have an opinion on goats. And probably everything else around here. You're just not willing to state it, because that would mean taking yourself off the sidelines of running the ranch." *And force you to take a stand on the family matters that are currently driving you crazy.*

Liz had been looking a little pale. At his unsolicited remark, color came rushing back into her face. She gave him a withering glare that made him smile, and set her briefcase down with a thud. Giving him a glance that told him she would deal with him later, in private, she pivoted back to her family. "You-all want to know what I think?"

The three women nodded, eager to hear.

"Years ago, when all four of us were working the

cattle together, we birthed a thousand calves a year and backgrounded another thousand more for other ranches. But that's not possible anymore. Because of the physical limitations we currently operate under, we've let the calving operation dwindle, and let our own backgrounding operation end entirely. We sell our cattle to another outfit as soon as they're weaned, at seven or eight months." She took a breath. "If we want the Four Winds to prosper the way it once did, we are going to have to build it back up. Take good care of all ten thousand acres, instead of just the ones we use. Like it or not, that involves bringing men into our operation. Full-time."

"Men are not part of Cartwright family tradition," Faye Elizabeth interrupted. "Not any who stay, anyway."

Triple ouch, Travis thought.

With a world of emotion in her low voice, Liz countered, "How well I know that. I love you all." Her lower lip trembled in a way that made him want to haul her into his arms and comfort her, audience or no audience.

Liz spread her arms wide. "I love the Four Winds. And I even love ranching—in small doses. But not enough to do it full-time. And that's not going to change."

Travis noted Reba's expression was extremely unhappy.

Faye Elizabeth was more accepting of the outburst, perhaps because she was by nature more of a pessimist. She shook her head. "I always knew it would come to this."

Travis thought having Liz finally speak her mind and stand up for herself was the best thing he'd heard in weeks.

Tillie rose and walked over to put her arm around Liz's shoulders. "Running a ranch has lost its allure in this day and age," she sympathized. "That I know."

"That may be true," Reba said. She turned to her only daughter. "And one day we may very well have to let our cattle raising operation go entirely."

Liz's expression gentled. "You wouldn't necessarily have to sell. There are other ways to make money from these ten thousand acres. We could give out hunting leases, for example."

Deciding to play devil's advocate, Travis added, "Or see if there is any oil to be had."

All four women stared at him.

Or maybe not...

Liz's great-grandmother stepped in, as only the matriarch of the family could. "There's no doubt we could change our whole way of life and still keep this property. But you would miss the Four Winds you grew up on," Tillie told Liz, with her usual romanticism.

A hint of melancholy tinged Liz's expression, even as she replied firmly, "The Four Winds will still be home to us, cattle or no cattle."

Her mother nodded. "Liz is right. Livestock isn't the issue here." Reba sent a speculative glance Travis's way. "What's really important is finding a way for her to have a baby to carry on the Cartwright name."

Send For
2 FREE BOOKS
Today!

I accept your offer!

Please send me two free
Harlequin American Romance®
novels and two mystery
gifts (gifts worth about $10).
I understand that these books
are completely free—even
the shipping and handling will
be paid—and I am under no
obligation to purchase anything, ever,
as explained on the back of this card.

154/354 HDL FMSH

© 2011 HARLEQUIN ENTERPRISES LIMITED. ® and ™ are trademarks owned and/or are trademarks owned by the trademark owner and/or its licensee. Printed in the U.S.A. ▲ Detach card and mail today. No stamp needed. ▲ H-AR-03/12

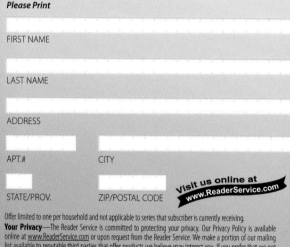

Please Print

FIRST NAME

LAST NAME

ADDRESS

APT.#   CITY

STATE/PROV.   ZIP/POSTAL CODE

**Visit us online at
www.ReaderService.com**

Offer limited to one per household and not applicable to series that subscriber is currently receiving.
Your Privacy—The Reader Service is committed to protecting your privacy. Our Privacy Policy is available online at www.ReaderService.com or upon request from the Reader Service. We make a portion of our mailing list available to reputable third parties that offer products we believe may interest you. If you prefer that we not exchange your name with third parties, or if you wish to clarify or modify your communication preferences, please visit us at www.ReaderService.com/consumerschoice or write to us at Reader Service Preference Service, P.O. Box 9062, Buffalo, NY 14269. Include your complete name and address.

The Reader Service—Here's how it works: Accepting your 2 free books and 2 free gifts (gifts valued at approximately $10.00) places you under no obligation to buy anything. You may keep the books and gifts and return the shipping statement marked "cancel." If you do not cancel, about a month later we'll send you 4 additional books and bill you just $4.49 each in the U.S. or $5.24 each in Canada. That is a savings of at least 14% off the cover price. It's quite a bargain! Shipping and handling is just 50¢ per book in the U.S. and 75¢ per book in Canada.* You may cancel at any time, but if you choose to continue, every month we'll send you 4 more books, which you may either purchase at the discount price or return to us and cancel your subscription.

*Terms and prices subject to change without notice. Prices do not include applicable taxes. Sales tax applicable in N.Y. Canadian residents will be charged applicable taxes. Offer not valid in Quebec. Credit or debit balances in a customer's account(s) may be offset by any other outstanding balance owed by or to the customer. Please allow 4 to 6 weeks for delivery. Offer available while quantities last. All orders subject to credit approval. Books received may not be as shown.

▼ If offer card is missing write to: The Reader Service, P.O. Box 1867, Buffalo, NY 14240-1867 or visit www.ReaderService.com ▼

NO POSTAGE
NECESSARY
IF MAILED
IN THE
UNITED STATES

BUSINESS REPLY MAIL
FIRST-CLASS MAIL   PERMIT NO. 717   BUFFALO, NY

POSTAGE WILL BE PAID BY ADDRESSEE

THE READER SERVICE
PO BOX 1867
BUFFALO NY 14240-9952

Chapter Nine

"You okay?"

Liz looked up to see Travis in the doorway of her private office. As usual whenever she caught sight of him, her heart gave a little leap. Not that he needed to know that. Especially after the way he had goaded her into speaking her mind to her family that very morning, when she already had her hands so full.

She tipped up her chin, trying not to notice how attractive Travis was at any time of day or night, with his dark brown hair and intent gray eyes. She reached for her bottle of mineral water and took a long sip. Pulse thudding, she regarded him over the rim, wondering how he knew just how to get to her. No matter what the situation...

"Why wouldn't I be?" she asked, wishing that her paralegal hadn't just left to pick up his son at day care, and that Travis hadn't arrived just in time to find her with her feet propped up on the desk, kicking back after a very busy and productive day.

"Oh, I don't know." He strolled on in, eyes falling to her polished toenails. "Maybe because your mom is nonstop in her efforts to get you to extend the Cartwright bloodlines?"

As graciously as possible, Liz swung her feet to the

floor. She tugged her skirt down and slipped on her heels. On warm days, when she didn't have to be in court, she didn't bother wearing panty hose. "You don't seem to mind."

He shook his head. "I get the same thing at home." He sat down on the corner of her desk, his twill work shirt taut across his shoulders, looser over his flat abs. His jeans gloved everything else perfectly.

"Although I have to admit…" Travis waggled his brows "…not quite as directly."

Liz pushed her chair backward, wheeling across the carpeted office floor to the built-in cabinet. Opening it, she pulled out another bottle of mineral water and handed it over.

After murmuring "thanks," he twisted off the cap and continued, "I suppose it's no surprise, since we're both unattached and of baby-making age."

She wheeled her chair back to her desk, and after taking another drink, he asked, "Do you want children?"

Another question she didn't expect. And normally would be inclined not to answer.

Something about the way he was looking at her prompted Liz to let down her guard. "Don't you dare tell my mom I said this, but yes, I do. When the time and man are right." Liz picked at a loose strip of label on her bottle. "What about you?" She reached beneath the desk and dropped the piece of paper into the trash.

Travis gazed at her candidly. "I want kids, too." A slow, sexy smile followed. "But like you…only when the time and the woman are right," he confided. "I'm not going to get hitched just because someone else thinks my biological clock should be ticking."

"Amen to that," Liz muttered, lifting her mineral water in salute.

Another contemplative silence fell. She pushed away the fantasy of one day making a baby with him. It wasn't going to happen. Not with Travis, anyway...

He'd be leaving soon.

Her expertise as a lawyer would ensure that.

"But that aside...surely that's not why you stopped by." Liz forged on, in an effort to get the conversation back on track.

Travis grimaced. "A vote was taken in your absence. I've been directed to purchase a dozen goats."

As if they didn't have enough livestock to care for already... Liz resisted the urge to bury her head in her hands and wail. "Angora or South African Boer?" she queried mildly.

Travis smiled at her, as if knowing exactly how beleaguered she felt. "Angora. Tillie likes mohair. Reba thinks they are easier to deal with than the meat-producing Boers."

Liz squared her shoulders. "Well...good luck. Glad I'm not involved." She stood to show him to the door.

Travis clamped a hand on her arm and turned her gently to face him. "Not so fast," he said, pushing a strand of hair from her cheek and tucking it behind her ear. "They want you to help me pick out the herd."

With her skin tingling where his warm palm grasped her elbow, Liz looked up at him. Whenever they were close like this, it was all she could do not to kiss him again.

She gulped, noticing how parched her throat felt. "No one else could do it?" she mused.

Travis frowned, not all that happy about the situation, either. "Apparently not. The good news is that the breeder is located about forty-five minutes north of town. So it won't take us long to get there."

Liz swept a hand to indicate her business suit and heels. "I'm not dressed for ranch activity."

Not about to let her off that easily, Travis smiled. "Exactly why your mom sent this." He went back into the reception area and returned with a small wheeled suitcase and a picnic basket.

So, Liz thought, the matchmaking was in full swing. "Dinner, too?"

He gestured aimlessly. "Although Faye Elizabeth didn't want us spending time alone together, she didn't want us going hungry, either."

Liz propped her hands on her hips, sensing something else at play here. "You could have talked them out of this, you know."

Travis let out a belly laugh that warmed the room. "Excuse me," he teased. "Have you *met* your family?"

Liz bowed her head. "Point made." Putting herself back on track, she asked, "What time is the goat ranch expecting us?"

"Seven."

"Which means we've got time." She picked up the items he'd brought and led him toward the break room, where a small table and chairs nestled next to the sink, fridge and cabinets. She handed him the wicker basket. "Set up here." Taking the suitcase with her, she said, "I'll be right back."

Travis did as ordered, and Liz walked in five minutes later, looking very sexy in a pair of faded jeans, boots and a marine-blue tank that appeared as if it had spent a few minutes too long in the clothes dryer.

"Don't say a word," she warned, lifting a hand.

His eyes sifted over the corset-style top and the lovely breasts spilling out of it. "I wasn't going to." Although damned if he wasn't getting aroused, just looking at her.

"My mother and Tillie got together and bought this for me for my birthday." Liz rummaged in the coat closet in the corner of the room.

Eventually, she emerged with a black cashmere cardigan, too warm for the spring day, and tugged it on.

"They were hoping it would spark something if I wore it to town on Saturday night."

I'll bet. Travis pushed away the surge of jealousy. "And have you?"

She returned his heated glance. "What do you think?"

"Not yet."

"Not at all," she confided, coming closer in a drift of jasmine perfume. "Although—as always—they both mean well."

Travis's body relaxed slightly as she buttoned the sweater. He nodded at the formfitting garment she was covering. "Bet Faye Elizabeth doesn't approve."

Liz snorted with laughter. "You bet right. But on to business…" She sat down opposite him, to the picnic dinner her grandmother had prepared for them. "Since we have a moment to talk…I got word about your case. And it's not good." Carefully, she removed the Saran Wrap covering her sandwich, admitting in a low, even tone, "Opposing counsel went ahead and filed the amendment to their petition against you, early this afternoon. So, as we agreed, I immediately filed an answer to the court, denying all charges. Plus a countersuit accusing HB&R of unlawful firing, and another defamation suit against Olympia Herndon."

Travis savored the delicious chicken and roasted green-chile wraps. "What next?"

Liz dipped a tortilla chip in freshly made salsa. "They want to depose you in Houston on Saturday morning. We asked to depose Olympia the same day."

Travis drank his iced tea. "That doesn't give us a lot of time to prepare. Just a few days." His cell phone buzzed. He lifted it out of his pocket, checked the caller and kept talking. "Especially for what is essentially going to be a 'he said, she said' case."

"We can do it. We'll start tonight." Liz finished the first half of her sandwich and dabbed her mouth with her napkin before leaning toward him. "If we get there and we're not ready, we'll request a delay."

Travis nodded. His phone buzzed again. He looked at the screen, frowned and put it back in his pocket without responding.

"You can get that if you want."

He shook his head in aggravation. "It's a nuisance call." A big nuisance.

Liz nodded, moving on. "Anyway," she said with a purposeful smile, "after we collect the goats, take them back to the ranch and get them situated, I'd like to meet up again—at the homestead—and start our prep."

Travis mentally ran through all they had to do regarding the goat herd. "It'll be late."

One corner of her mouth turned up in an ironic smile that reached her pretty green eyes. "I won't turn into a pumpkin before midnight, I promise."

His phone buzzed yet again. Trying not to cuss, Travis pulled the device out of his shirt pocket. To his relief, he saw a different caller this time.

He looked at Liz. "It's your great-grandmother. I've got to take it."

Liz moaned and got up to clear the remains of their picnic.

"Hey, Tillie. Yes, I talked Liz into going with me."

Liz mouthed playfully, *"With one arm twisted behind my back."*

Travis grinned as he listened to the older woman's complicated reminders, regarding what they wanted and needed for optimum land management.

What she had to say next, however, was not welcome news.

LIZ DIDN'T KNOW what was going on at the other end of the connection, but Travis's mood turned from jovial to somber in an instant.

"Okay, thanks for telling me," he said eventually. "I'm not sure how long I'll be. I'd appreciate that...." He paused again. "Not to worry. You did the right thing."

Right thing about what? Liz wondered. And why did he suddenly look so piqued? "Trouble?"

He shook his head, without quite looking her in the eye. "Another nuisance."

Hmm. "You sure have a lot of those today," Liz commented.

He shrugged and started to help clean up after their picnic. "Comes with the territory," he muttered, suddenly in a hurry to be on their way. "What do you say we go buy the goats and load 'em up in the livestock hauler, and then I'll drop you back here at the office, so you can pick up your car."

Liz knew there was no reason to take two vehicles all the way out to the goat ranch, when they could easily save on gas and leave one in town. "Sounds good to me."

Fortunately, the animals up for sale were all in prime

condition. Liz and Travis picked out a dozen, and minutes later, the bill of sale was completed. The goats were herded into the livestock trailer attached to Travis's truck, and they headed back to town again.

"Everything okay?" Liz asked him. Something was obviously going on.

He stared out the windshield. "Why do you ask?"

Why had she? Usually, she wasn't this nosy. Finally, Liz made a noncommittal sound, then stated, "You seem tense." Really tense.

And that wasn't like him.

Usually he was very confident, laid-back.

It was his turn to be noncommittal.

Travis shrugged as the cell phone in his pocket went off once again. This time he didn't even look at it.

So, Liz thought, something *was* going on. Something he preferred she not know about.

She wondered if it had anything to do with his defense, or the legal answer and lawsuits they had just filed.

Because if so...

Liz took in his rugged profile as his cell phone went off once more. "Hey. If you want to pull over and get that..."

His jaw set. "Nope."

O-kay.

They reached the parking lot of her office. Travis swore when he saw the black SUV with tinted windows pulled up in front, motor running.

As he parked, a uniformed chauffeur stepped out from behind the wheel. He opened the back passenger door. A white-haired gentleman known throughout the Texas energy community stepped out.

Liz recognized him from his pictures, which were

often in the business section of Texas newspapers. Hargett Anderson.

He held out a hand, gripped hers firmly. "You must be Liz Cartwright," he said.

Liz smiled, returning the firm handshake. She looked into his intelligent eyes, so much like Travis's. "And you must be Travis's grandfather."

"That I am," he said proudly. "Although—" he turned to frown at his grandson "—you would never know it by the way he refuses to return my emails and phone calls."

Travis scowled, a muscle working in his jaw. "Liz doesn't need to be in the middle of this, Grandpa Hargett."

Hargett harrumphed. "She wouldn't be, if you'd been at the Four Winds, where you were supposed to be this evening."

Travis opened up the hauler to let air in and check on the goats, in their large, steel travel crates. Seeing Travis, they let out a chorus of indignant baas.

"I'm not discussing this here," he said.

Hargett shook his head in disgust at the goats, then turned back to his grandson. "Then I'll do the talking. It's time you put all your knowledge to good use and come to work for Anderson Oil as my protégé."

Travis tensed all the more. "I have no interest in being an executive."

"Do what I tell you and one day you'll be running the place," he pressed.

Travis let out a short, impatient breath. "You tried this on Dad. It didn't work there and it won't work on me. Now…if you don't mind, Grandpa Hargett, I've got goats to transport."

Hargett Anderson stared at his grandson. "You're

serious," he said finally. "All that education. Editor of *Texas Law Review* at the University of Texas. And this is what you've been reduced to!"

SINCE THEY DROVE separate vehicles back to the ranch, Liz had no chance to find out what Travis was thinking or feeling. And once there, of course, they had work to do.

"You did a great job of picking out the goats," Tillie exclaimed, as Liz helped Travis get the last of the dozen angora goats into the pasture closest to the barn and put out supplemental feed and water.

Reba nodded in approval, too. She watched a tall female dubbed Queenie—for her propensity of becoming herd queen, no matter what group of angoras she was placed in—roam the pasture, her horned head held high.

On the other side of the herd was the lone male, dubbed Buck, for obvious reasons.

The other goats hadn't been named.

Liz wasn't sure they would give them monikers. At least not right away.

Tillie shook her head in admiration at the flock. "White, charcoal, beige and blue-gray. They're beautiful, Liz and Travis. Just beautiful."

It was true, Liz thought. The horned animals had fluffy, full coats. "They'll need shearing in another month," she said.

Faye Elizabeth beamed. "It's been a while since we did that. It'll really give us a chance to work together as a team."

Which was, Liz thought guiltily, something they rarely did anymore.

Reba turned to Travis. "Given that this was your first experience with goats, what did you think?"

Oh, no, Liz thought. *Don't answer.*

Goat herding on cattle ranches was more of a lady rancher thing. Men preferred driving big expensive tractors for land management.

Travis, bless his heart, considered carefully before replying. "I'm thinking you should probably follow the breeder's advice and get a couple of guard donkeys to scare off predators, when you do put them out in the far pastures."

"Not a bad idea," Tillie said. "I'll get to work on researching that this evening."

More conversation followed and then the other women headed back to the house.

Liz turned to Travis. He had been a good sport so far. Unable to help herself, she said playfully, "Not exactly what you had in mind when you offered to be the Four Winds's only cowboy, is it? Even temporarily."

He snorted in laughter. Rubbed the muscles at the back of his neck. "Life is full of surprises."

"Like your grandfather's visit?"

Travis straightened the brim of his hat, dragging it lower. "I knew that was coming. I was just hoping to avoid it."

Glancing at the setting sun and the vivid streaks of red and pink in the blue-gray sky, Liz asked, "You're really not interested in being groomed by Hargett to one day run Anderson Oil?"

Travis lounged against the wooden fence, observing the goats. "I don't belong in a CEO's office, Liz. I like writing contracts. Solving technical legal problems. Not chasing down energy sources."

Liz could see that. Could see a lot of things when Travis opened up to her this way.

He took in the breathtaking vista of the Four Winds, confiding quietly, "My dad felt the same way. He was so dead set against it that he hid the fact he was heir to a large oil company."

Liz had heard that story; it was the stuff of Laramie County legends.

"My dad was so determined to be his own man, as a matter of fact, that he took a ranch job with the Mc-Cabes, while saving up the money to start his own operation."

Liz considered the irony. "And now you're hiding out and working on our ranch."

"Not quite the same thing. My dad's exodus was entirely voluntary."

"Whereas you're stuck," Liz concluded, not sure how she felt about that.

"Only temporarily," Travis corrected. He reached over and playfully tugged on a strand of her hair, the way he had when they were younger. He paused to look deep into her eyes, intensifying the intimacy between them. "I'm relying on you to get the lawsuit against me dropped and my license reinstated sooner than anyone thinks."

"WE DON'T HAVE TO DO THIS tonight, if you don't want," Liz told Travis an hour later, when she walked into the homestead. He'd been on the go since dawn, as had she, and it was nearly ten o'clock.

Freshly showered, but not shaved, he shrugged. "May as well get it over with. Besides, along with everything else I have to do tomorrow, I hear I'm going to be picking up a couple of jackasses. If they can find the perfect ones, anyway. I'm told that can be a little harder than locating goats."

"That's true." Liz grinned, glad he was starting to find the humor in the situation. "Although I'm sure the ladies would prefer you use the term guard donkeys instead of jackasses." She drew a breath. "Sorry this gig hasn't turned out the way you envisioned it."

His gray eyes twinkled. "Are you kidding? This is exactly how I figured working for four Cartwright women would be. Peppered with a little fighting and a lot of meddling...and some highly unusual requests." He exhaled slowly. "Not to mention a lot of very fine dining, and plenty of peace and quiet in which to think—if you can discount the occasional mooing of a lovesick cow or the bleating of some ticked-off goats being shuffled around."

"Well, as long as you have your sense of humor intact...!"

Liz opened her laptop computer and retrieved the file of questions she had prepared earlier in the day. "Let's get to it." She met his eyes. "Did you and Olympia ever sign a disclosure agreement about your relationship?"

Cocking his head, he studied her for a long moment. "I didn't think it would be necessary."

"So you didn't even offer it up as a possibility," Liz surmised.

Annoyance flickered across his features. "I did."

Her fingers hovered above the keyboard. "Before or after you got involved?"

His attitude turned matter-of-fact. "We were only together for about four weeks."

Having met Olympia, Liz was surprised it had gone on that long. "Was this before or after you were representing her?"

"It started just before she asked me to and signed with our law firm."

Curious, Liz paused. "Did you know she was interested in signing with HB&R at the point you became intimately involved?"

"I knew she was thinking about it. She had asked to look at the standard client-attorney representation forms from the firm. Basically, she wanted to know what the services were, what my billing rate versus that of one of the senior partners was, and so on." He shrugged. "She was supposed to come into the office to discuss it, but she'd twisted her ankle playing tennis and couldn't drive, so I went to her place."

Liz pushed away her emotional reaction to his naivete. "Alone," she specified casually.

Travis nodded. "It was kind of a spur-of-the-moment thing. She asked me to pick up a prescription for her at the pharmacy."

Liz stifled a groan of dismay. "Tell me it wasn't pain medicine."

"It was pain medicine. But she didn't take any while I was there, because she was drinking wine and knew better than to mix the two."

"Will she testify to that?" Liz pressed.

Looking momentarily dejected, he shook his head, indicating he didn't know.

Forging on, Liz said gently, "Tell me what happened when you got there."

"She was on the sofa. She had her leg propped up on some pillows, and her ankle was packed in ice."

"Did she seem to be in pain?"

"Initially, yes," he replied.

"But as the evening wore on?"

Travis grimaced. "This is going to sound really dumb."

Liz waited.

"She said she couldn't climb the stairs. She asked me to carry her up to bed."

"And you did?"

"I knew it was over-the-top dramatic," he admitted. "But I was raised to be a gentleman."

"And you were both single."

"Very single. So…when we got to her bed and she invited me to stay…I did."

This was the sticking point. "Because you wanted to sign her as a client."

"No." Travis's tone was flat, unequivocal. "I would have given that up to have a relationship with her. I still intended to bring her into the firm, if at all possible, because I knew it was a big deal and I'd get credit for it."

Liz nodded, seeing where this was going, from a professional perspective. "You could have made your disclosure and handed over her business to one of the founding partners…."

"Right. But she wanted me as her lawyer. And she wanted an ongoing relationship with me."

Liz knew how ambitious Travis was, how pressured by at least some of his family to succeed. Particularly in light of his refusing to join Anderson Oil.

She sympathized with what a dilemma it must have been. Olympia offering him the world, Travis eager to gain acceptance into the firm. "Did you have any qualms about it?"

"Not at the time," he admitted honestly. "Looking back, I probably should have. But she didn't think it would impact our working together, and we agreed to keep our relationship private."

"So you brought her into the firm, as your client," Liz said.

"And my bosses at the firm were delighted, because she was an excellent businesswoman, and an heiress to an oil fortune who was ready to strike out on her own. She was also going to be a pretty big client. There was only one catch."

Again Liz waited.

"She wanted a lower billing rate for all her business."

Liz paused. "I didn't think Haverty, Brockman & Roberts ever did that."

Travis exhaled. "They don't. But it was going to be a deal breaker, so I kept working on them, and finally was able to convince my bosses that the volume of business Olympia was going to bring in, as she built her oil operation from the ground up, would more than offset any loss. And since it was my rate being cut, not theirs, they finally agreed."

Liz thought about what a coup that must have been for Travis. "Olympia was happy, I'm guessing?"

He nodded. "Ecstatic—in terms of business."

"And personally?"

"She began to lose interest in us almost immediately."

If Travis was heartbroken, Liz noted, he sure wasn't showing it. "So you stopped seeing each other."

"And sleeping together," he clarified.

Liz paused, adding two and two, not just from an attorney's perspective, but a woman's. "Has it occurred to you that Olympia—"

"—only hopped into bed with me and stayed there until she got her lower billing rate?" Travis asked sagely. "Yes. It has."

So he knew he'd been duped. And was accepting responsibility where it was due. Learning from his mistakes. Moving on. Liz couldn't help but admire him for that. It would have been very easy for him, under the circumstances, to assuage all blame, become bitter, angry, lash out.

"Did you work harder for her, after that?" she asked quietly.

Travis put the kibosh on that notion. "I gave my client the best of my ability, same as always."

No more, no less.

Liz sat back in her chair and studied him. She felt she already knew the answers to these questions, but had to ask them nevertheless. "Were you hoping Olympia would take you back, if you were successful on her behalf?"

Again, there wasn't the slightest bit of indecision on his face. "No."

A mixture of relief and respect flowed through Liz. "Why not?" she asked, even more quietly. Restless, she stood and moved away from her computer.

"Because I realized a sexual affair wasn't enough." Travis stood, too, and came toward her. "I wanted more from a relationship." His voice dropped another husky notch and his eyes darkened. "I wanted what I once had, with you."

Chapter Ten

Liz hitched in a breath at the words she had longed to hear. She took a nervous step back. Memories of the way he had kissed her the last time they'd faced off like this sent a burning flame throughout her entire body. Wary of leaping in too soon, too fast, she lifted a palm. "Travis. We promised this wasn't going to happen again."

Something hot and sensual shimmered in his eyes. He caught her hand in his and came closer still. "*You* said that." He slipped an arm around her waist. "*I've* been holding on to hope that it would."

She flushed, heating at the intoxicating feel of him pressed against her.

Liz tilted her head back. "You realize mixing pleasure and legal representation is what got you into trouble before."

His intelligent gray eyes sparked with sheer male determination. "Pursuing pleasure minus any real feeling or commitment is what got me in trouble before." Travis sifted his fingers through her hair. "Now I have both." He paused to gaze intently into her eyes, before adding quietly, "We stopped short of where we should have gone before, and it was the single biggest mistake of my life."

His unexpected declaration sent emotion bubbling up inside her, and Liz swallowed. There was no harm in talking honestly, was there? "Mine, too."

His eyelids lowered and he gave her a light, tender kiss. "So let's make a promise here and now," he coaxed softly. "Let's not do that again…."

Liz had told herself there would be no more hot, passionate, wildly out-of-control kisses between them. That no matter how intimate the conversation or situation became, she would be smart and restrained. That vow fled the moment he kissed her again.

It wasn't so much the possessive feel of his mouth or the way he slid his tongue over her lower lip.

It was the way he took charge and dominated the moment—and her. The way he made her feel so ravished and cherished all at once.

"Travis…" She caught her breath. Tried to be strong.

"Liz…" Mocking her playfully, he shifted his hands to her spine, molding her against him so there was no mistaking his desire, or the pounding of his heart beneath his shirt. No mistaking the cavalcade of feelings roaring through her, or the dampness gathering between her thighs.

Her fingers were in his hair. Holding him at bay or bringing him close? All she knew was that the dark strands were soft and thick and silky.

"You're impossible." She pushed out the words.

He grinned at the defiant edge. "Determined," he corrected, rubbing his thumb across her lips. "And yes," he agreed with sexy confidence that made her hormones surge, "I am…."

He turned his attention to her lips again, kissing her ardently. The stubble on his jaw felt deliciously masculine rubbing against her face, and she inhaled deeply, breathing him in.

Leather. Soap. Man.

Power.

Lust.

So much lust.

Groaning in desperation, Liz turned her head. "We shouldn't use sex to escape from our problems...."

Not the least bit dissuaded, Travis nuzzled the side of her neck, finding the nerve endings just below her ear. "How about we use sex for our pleasure then?"

If only it could be that simple, Liz thought wistfully. But it couldn't.

She moaned as he cupped her hips, pressing her intimately against him, until she could feel her whole body swaying as she succumbed to yet another slow, sultry kiss.

He responded in kind and Liz slid her hands up his arms, enjoying the feel of his biceps, so warm and solid, beneath her palms. "Because pleasure isn't uncomplicated."

She sighed again as he divested her of her shirt and murmured, "It can be."

Her nipples beaded against her bra, begging to be touched. "Not," she gasped, "when feelings are involved."

His lips found her breasts. His thumbs gently caressed her bared belly, making her muscles quiver. "Are there feelings involved here?"

A shiver went through her and Liz shut her eyes against the overwhelming pleasure. "How can there not be? I care about you."

He flashed her a lopsided grin. "And I care about you."

Heaven help me. "As friends."

Something flickered in his eyes at that. Something she couldn't read. Didn't want to read…

Studying her noncommittally, he leaned in and kissed her again. "Friends can have sex."

Liz put a hand on his chest, not sure if she was stopping him or inviting him to come closer. She hitched in another breath as her nipples hardened all the more. "Not if they're smart, they don't."

And I'm a liar, because I want you. So much.

He grinned, the twinkle in his eyes igniting all her erogenous zones. Mischievously, he reached behind her and undid the clasp on her bra. He viewed her rapaciously, making her feel beautiful. "Stop thinking of reasons why not to be together." He dropped his head and dragged his lips across her collarbone, to the inner curves of her breasts.

She could feel him, hard and ready. "I'm just trying to help us…"

He kissed her again and turned her, pushing her back against the wall, freeing his hands for other things. Such as undoing the zipper on her jeans. "You're trying to ignore what we feel."

Liz shut her eyes as he found her there, too. *Oh my.* She rubbed up against him, taking what he gave, soaking in the feel of him, his scent. "Which is?"

"Lust." He stroked her softly. "Friendship." Going deeper still. "Compassion."

The mind-blowing intimacy of his touch had her arching in pleasure. On the brink, Liz drew in a shaky breath. She should push him away. Instead, she pressed herself against him, still kissing, wanting more. Knowing all the while he was missing the most important thing.

Liz caught his face in her hands, looked deep into his eyes and in a throaty whisper added her own analysis of what it was they were both searching to find. "And...a yearning to go backward in time to when things were so much simpler."

His rich laugh washed over her like a sweet caress, a kiss. "Things *are* simple."

"Since when?" she asked with a rough exhalation of breath, her heart suddenly in her throat.

He dipped his head and rubbed his lips across her temple. "Since I want you and you want me, and we both wish we hadn't been apart all these years." His voice was raw. Persuasive. He kissed her again, until she met him stroke for stroke, parry for parry, keeping her focus on the ultimate goal. "Let go of your defenses, Liz. Of your rules and restrictions and plans for the future..." His big body cradled her tenderly. "Let life just happen to you for a little bit...."

She searched his face. "Is that what we're doing?"

His eyes darkened. "It sure as heck is what I'm doing...."

And what he wanted from her, too.

He opened the snaps on his shirt and yanked her to him, so her bare breasts pressed against the hardness of his chest. In the feminine heart of her, she could feel the tingling.

"But—"

He pushed down her jeans, then his. "No buts. No talking. Nothing but this..."

Nothing but the pleasure he was giving her and she was giving him.

Then they were kissing again and he was lifting her and the sensation of being filled by him stole her breath. She couldn't get enough of him. The hardness. The tenderness. She tried to set the pace, but he held her right where he wanted, right where she needed to be. Desire swept through her, turning to a deep, all-encompassing need. She pressed herself closer, letting the world spiral out of control as she savored every intoxicating kiss, and each slow, fierce, deliberate thrust.

They moved together, surrendering to each other, to these feelings, to whatever this was, Liz thought with a contented sigh, and would be.

FROM THE WALL, they moved to the bed, where Travis made love to Liz all over again. Afterward, he cuddled her close, savoring the soft femininity of her body. "I meant what I said. I want us to commit to an ongoing..." He searched for the proper word and, because nothing would actually suffice, lamely came up with, "...thing."

Liz lifted her head and studied him with vulnerable eyes. "You mean a relationship, at least of sorts."

He wanted a hell of a lot more than that. He wanted to know she was his, and he was hers. But he had already pushed her too fast and too hard by seducing her back into bed with him, without giving them a chance to get their lives sorted out first, so he nodded.

Looking wary, and maybe a little panicked again, just as he had feared, Liz disentangled herself from his arms and stiffly rose to her feet. "I'm not sure we should enter into a relationship at this time."

Could she sound—or act—more lawyerly? He saw the emotional force field go up around her, effectively shutting him out. Knew he'd do anything to break down the barrier that kept them apart. "Why not?"

She wrapped the blanket around her and perched on the edge of the bed. Briefly, she closed her eyes. "I'm all for exclusivity—for now, but beyond that..."

His emotions in turmoil, Travis rose and pulled her against him, stilling her restless movements. He ran his hand up her arm, over her shoulder, not stopping until it rested beneath the thick, silky fall of her hair at her nape.

She locked eyes with him. "You're in the middle of a crisis. You're relying on me to help get you out of it, the same way I'm counting on you to help my family manage the ranch."

Frustration gathered like a fist inside him. "So we need each other." He slid a possessive hand down her spine and felt her tremble. "So what?"

Her eyes revealed her responses but she lifted a shoulder, feigning indifference. "So…once your law license is reinstated, you're not going to need me anymore."

He studied the rosy hue of her cheeks, knowing he was already halfway to where he wanted to be. Halfway home. "But you'll still need *me,*" he pointed out casually.

She looked miserable and resigned—a rarity for her. "We'll find another ranch hand, Travis. Maybe even a lady wrangler, if it will make 'the ladies' happy."

He threaded his fingers through her hair. Tilted her head back and waited until she looked directly at him again.

"And I'll still want you…. And you'll still want me, no matter how much you deny it."

Liz shook her head sadly and splayed her hands across his chest, forcing distance between them. "What you're going to want to do," she corrected, "is resign from your job on the Four Winds and resume your career." Determination lit her eyes. "And I'll support you in that decision, because it will be the right thing."

Selflessness had gotten her exactly nowhere. Travis knew, because it had landed him in the very same place. He backed her to the bed and fell down onto it with her. Deciding that talking was useless right now, he kissed her again, sliding his hands beneath her hips and lifting her until she was arching against him.

"I'm not going back to Houston," he said with a calm he wasn't close to feeling.

Liz bit her lip. "Maybe you will and maybe you won't," she replied, even as she wrapped her arms around him. "The point is, you're a talented attorney and you will land somewhere, Travis. When that happens, you'll leave Laramie County and this ranch. And our affair will be all over." Her breath hitched. "But I'm okay with that."

He lifted a mocking brow. "You are?"

She nodded. "I have to be." A mixture of sorrow and acceptance laced her voice. "We both do."

"Because...?" he prodded, ignoring the thudding of his pulse.

"We're grown-ups. And adults deal with the way things are, not the way we wish they were." Liz smiled briefly and slid her fingers through his hair. "But that doesn't mean, since we've started this—" she tenderly kissed a corner of his mouth, then the center "—that we can't enjoy each other now...."

LIZ TOLD HERSELF she was diverting him, distracting them both, really, for fear that he would discover how much he meant to her. Yet everything she'd told Travis was true.

They couldn't fall in love. They could take the risk of being together and enjoy each other—for now.

Beyond that it was foolish to think.

So she gave their lovemaking her all. When they were done, she lay spent, wrapped in his arms. "I've got to go...."

"I know." He held her tighter.

"And I will." Just as soon as her breathing slowed... and her heart resumed a normal beat.

The next thing Liz knew, sunlight was streaming in through the windows. She jerked awake. "Oh, no. No, no, no!"

Travis swore. Sat up and looked around, as disoriented and disheveled as she.

"I can't believe I spent the whole night here!"

Momentarily, Travis looked pleased. Then he grasped the ramifications of what they had done and swore again.

Liz glanced at the alarm that hadn't gone off—probably because it hadn't been set, she noted wryly. "Seven o'clock." She clapped a hand to her forehead. "That means they're all up!"

"They're going to be upset?"

"*I'm* upset!" Liz vaulted from the bed and scrambled to find her clothes. "I haven't had to do a walk of shame since...well, since never. I like keeping my private life private, and that goes double for my mother and grandmothers."

Travis got up and began to dress hurriedly, too. He grimaced, all chivalrous male. "This is my fault."

She put her shirt on. Realized it was inside out and tried again. "You didn't cause me to fall asleep." She looked down as she buttoned.

He sauntered closer, pulling his own shirt on. "I made love with you until we were both exhausted," he pointed out with a hint of a smile.

Liz slapped at the hand he ran down her hip. "Stop distracting me."

He grinned, not all that repentant. "Sorry."

Liz sat on the bed and thrust her feet into her boots. "I don't know what I'm going to say."

"Say nothing."

Liz's head snapped up. "What?"

"You stay put," he ordered firmly, already striding for the exit. "I'll go."

"What?" Liz did a double take. "Why would you want to do that?"

Guilt flashed in his eyes. "Because if there are consequences from our tryst, they should be mine."

Giving her no chance to protest, he took off to handle it the way he thought it should be handled.

IT WAS AS BAD AS LIZ had feared it would be. As he approached the ranch house, voices floated out of the open window over the kitchen sink. "Maybe we should look for her at the homestead..."

"Her car is still here."

"And her bed hasn't been slept in."

So they knew that, too.

Bracing himself, Travis walked in. All three women turned to look at him. Too late, he realized it might have been better if he had shaved or combed his hair. Tucked in his shirttail. But since he hadn't...

He lifted a hand. "There is no cause to worry, ladies. Liz is fine. She's at the homestead. We were working late last night. She fell asleep and I didn't bother to wake her."

"Don't go parsing any words or playing those lawyer tricks on me, young man," Faye Elizabeth said. "You've been romancing my granddaughter!"

No use denying it. They were all intuitive enough to sense how he felt. "Yes, ma'am. I have," he said, and left it at that.

At his admission, Tillie flashed an encouraging smile. She walked over to slap him on the shoulder. "Atta boy. You go after my great-granddaughter with all you've got."

Travis dipped his head respectfully. "Yes, ma'am."

Reba studied him a long silent moment. "Given the fact I'd do anything to have a grandbaby, I hope you weren't too careful!"

"Mom, please!" Liz exclaimed as she walked in the screen door, looking only slightly less disheveled than Travis. All eyes turned to her. She blushed to the roots of her hair, and Travis decided she looked prettier than he had ever seen her.

"You don't have to suffer through this. I'll take it from here," she told him.

"We're in this together," he said.

"I like the sound of that even more!" Reba declared.

"Well, I don't." Faye Elizabeth waved a finger at Liz. "There is no reason this gentleman's excess of testosterone should be your problem. Let him sow his wild seeds elsewhere!"

Liz tossed her hair. "I've got testosterone, too, you know. All women do."

Were they really talking about male hormones?

Travis didn't find out, because just then the phone rang. It was for Liz. J.T. was about to be arrested again. She looked around for her purse and keys. "I've got to go," she said. "None of you discuss any of this in my absence!"

An order, Travis found out, that was easier said than done.

LIZ HAD NO TROUBLE finding her client. He was standing in the street holding a big sign attached to a wooden stake. She rushed toward him. "J.T., you cannot picket city hall."

A deputy watched from a distance.

J.T. scowled. "Why not?"

She took his arm and guided him into the shade next to the limestone building. "You need a permit. You do not have one."

His shoulders sagged, and he looked at her in misery. "I want that pool. I don't see why it's taking so long for the zoning commission to come up with a plan. It's all I can think about."

Liz soothed, "These things take time. They're working on it as we speak, I promise."

J.T. looked skeptical.

"In the meantime," Liz said, as her next idea hit, "what do you know about donkeys?"

Her client peered at her suspiciously. "Is this a roundabout way of calling me a jackass? Because if it is..."

She shook her head. "It's a roundabout way of asking if you would be amenable to helping my mother go pick out a couple of donkeys to guard the angora goats we just bought."

J.T. took a moment to digest the request. "Isn't that Travis's job, since he's your hired hand?"

Liz made a face. "If you want to know the truth, Travis is not all that keen on goats or donkeys. He's more of a cattleman. Besides, I have some other things I need him to do. So what do you say?" She stepped closer, appealing to the retired gentleman's softer side. "Can the ladies and I count on you?"

J.T. rubbed the back of his bald head. "I guess I do

owe you-all for that nice dinner the other night," he said finally.

Liz smiled. "Then how about coming back to the ranch with me right now?"

To her relief, he agreed, and half an hour later they were both at the Four Winds. Liz situated J.T. in the kitchen with the ladies, so a search for two donkeys could be made via phone and internet. Then she went looking for Travis.

She found him in the south pasture, in a brand-new utility tractor with a bulldozer bucket on the front and a grader on the back. She parked the ranch pickup and got out.

He cut the engine, climbed down and came toward her. Stubble lined his handsome jaw. His shirt clung to the muscles of his chest and sweat dripped from his brow, under the brim of his hat.

"That doesn't look like our tractor." It had the Double Deal Ranch logo on the side, which meant he'd borrowed it from his folks.

Travis shrugged. "The Four Winds tractor can't handle a job like this one."

No kidding. Liz surveyed what he'd done with an admiring glance. "You've already cleared half the pasture." She'd had no idea they made tractors this efficient. Or from the looks of it, so easy to use. But then, she hadn't done much investigating about what kind of equipment they could get to help the ranch run more efficiently.

"What are you thinking?"

"One, that I have to figure out what kind of rental fee we're going to give your parents for the use of this utility tractor. And two, that I haven't exactly done my part in trying to figure out how to help keep the Four

Winds in our family for the next generation of women, and the one after that."

He tipped back his hat and flashed her a flirtatious grin. "You say that as if you think there won't be any men here."

Awareness sizzled through her. "It is tradition."

"A tradition that needs to be broken."

Liz pretended to misunderstand. "You really think J.T. and my mother might be a good match?"

Travis caught her by the waist and hauled her close, sweat and all. "I think *you and I* are a good match."

He spread hot, openmouthed kisses along her throat, then her jaw, testing the sweet spot beneath her ear before finally ending up at her lips. Liz leaned into him, savoring the salty taste of him, the dampness of his shirt, the hard male feel of his body and the minty taste of his tongue.

"You are," she breathed, amazed at his ability to get her off track, even with the hot sun bearing down on them, "so bad for me...."

Travis grinned. "Actually, we're good for each other." He delivered another deep, soul-searching kiss. "Really good."

Much more, and they'd be taking it to the max, right here in this field. Liz splayed her hands across his chest. "Travis..."

He lifted his head. "Don't worry. I'll get these pastures cleared." Gently, he caressed her face.

Another spiral of desire wound through her. Liz cleared her throat. "I don't question that. In just two hours you did..." She paused, looked around admiringly.

"What it would take those goats a month to do," he finished.

Liz scoffed. "You make fun, but goats do clear the land if you don't have the budget for a big, new tractor like that." Which would, she knew, cost thousands and thousands of dollars.

For the moment, anyway, they were just going to have to make do, and Travis would have to accept that. Not that he would be here for long, anyway.

"Speaking of guard donkeys…"

He quirked his lips. "Were we?"

Liz looked at him archly. "I've got some good news about that. My mother and J.T. are going to purchase them and bring them back in the livestock hauler. Unlike with the goats, all you'll have to do is help unload."

Travis shook his head. "Then let's hope they're friendly jackasses."

Indeed. Liz promised, "I'll find out what we need to do to keep from getting kicked."

He looked as if he wanted to kiss her again, so she stepped back. "Meanwhile, I need you to construct a time line and put together any supporting evidence regarding your relationship with Olympia Herndon."

Travis's smile faded. "I'll see what I can do to come up with a paper trail," he said gruffly. "But I won't be able to get to it until later this evening."

"That's okay." Liz paused, knowing they had one more item to discuss. "About this morning and the brouhaha with the ladies. Thanks for trying to save me, but it really wasn't necessary."

"You're my woman." He hauled her into his arms, all signs of teasing gone. "You've earned my defense, and a whole lot more."

Chapter Eleven

"You haven't heard a word we said," Reba said that evening.

Liz looked up from her plate. Everyone else was nearly finished with dinner. She had barely made a dent in hers.

"What are you thinking about, dear?" Tillie asked gently.

"Work," Liz fibbed. And the man sitting opposite her, in the ranch house dining room. *Was* she Travis's woman? Was he her man? She knew he wanted to be, at least for now. But what did she want…?

Peace of mind, for starters. Assurance that he would stay in her life this time, if—and it was a big if—she ever gave him her heart.

Right now, they should be focused on building his defense and on working the ranch, and instead they were having sex.

Along that path lay disaster. She knew it. He knew it. Even her family knew it. The only person at the table who was unaware of the jeopardy Liz and Travis were in was J.T.

After a day spent chasing down leads on guard donkeys, the widower looked happier than he had for ages. Even though no decision had been made.

"Speaking of work," Travis said, "I've got a lot to get done tonight, too. And frankly, Liz, I could use your help organizing the papers you asked me to produce."

The idea of spending time alone with him caused a riot of sensations inside her. Not a good idea, she knew, when she was still trying to sort out her feelings.

On the other hand, the deposition was on Friday.

She toyed with her last bite of barbecued chicken. Travis cocked an eyebrow, waiting for her response. "What about the goats?" she said finally.

"If you'll lend us the dogs to help round them up," Reba said with a coy wink. "J.T. and I will bring them in from the pasture."

Travis's head dipped in easy acquiescence. "Sure thing."

"Anyone want dessert?" Tillie asked, eager to get the show on the road.

"If it's okay, I'll take mine to go," Travis said.

Of course you will, Liz thought, eyeing the luscious desserts her great-grandmother brought to the table.

Tillie picked up the server. "Pecan pie or apple dumpling?"

"How about a little of both?" he suggested.

"You got it. Liz?"

"No, thanks. I'm on a diet." *A no-more-sex-until-I-straighten-out-the-rest-of-my-life diet.*

Travis looked at her, then pushed back his chair and rose. "I'll bring the dogs over. Ladies? The meal was delicious as always." He flashed Liz another grin, then left.

She released the breath she hadn't realized she was holding, then got up to help clear the table, not at all surprised to find her knees were wobbly.

"How is his situation coming along?" Tillie asked sympathetically.

Not as good as it would be if I was less emotionally involved. Careful not to violate client confidentiality, Liz said, "Okay. But he's right…we have a lot of work to do."

Liz looked at her other client. "Which isn't to say I haven't done a lot for you, too, today, J.T. If all goes as promised, we should have a proposal to show you by tomorrow afternoon."

"I'll look forward to it," J.T. said agreeably.

Rising, he pulled out her mother's chair and held the back door open for her. The two walked out after Travis, their movements perfectly in sync despite Reba's lingering sciatica.

Liz did her best not to visibly react. His gallantry probably meant nothing, since J.T. was of a different generation. He'd been lamenting his wife's passing just the day before, and couldn't possibly be feeling anything for her mother. Nothing that wasn't strictly in rebound territory, anyway.

Liz wondered if her mom knew about rebound romances.

Tillie tsked and swatted Liz's hand when she tried to clear more than her own dishes. "You go on and help Travis, honey. Don't want to keep a good man waiting."

Faye Elizabeth tightened her lips, concerned as always. "A little waiting might be good for that fellow."

Liz winced as telltale heat spread across her face. Deciding to take this particular bull by the horns, she looked into her grandmother's worried eyes. "You don't have to be concerned, Gran. I can handle whatever comes my way."

"You be sure of that." Faye Elizabeth patted her arm.

"Because like I said this morning, his hormones aren't your problem, and vice versa."

Yes, but the way I want him, and no longer want to be without him, is *my problem.*

"THAT WAS FAST." Travis let her into the homestead.

In the distance, Liz could see her mother and J.T. headed in the direction of the pasture where the goats had spent the day, the two dogs trotting at their sides.

Shrugging, she walked through the door. The cabin that had been hers until recently now was thoroughly a man's domain, with a Texas Rangers baseball game playing on the TV. Clothing tossed everywhere. The smell of soap and aftershave lingering in the air.

"I got kicked out of the kitchen and hurried on over here."

He turned to her, his eyes eating her up, before he shut the door. "Over your protests, I'm guessing."

"Because of my indiscreet behavior this morning, we're under the microscope now."

He stepped closer. "First of all, it wasn't just your behavior. It was ours. Second," he murmured, his breath brushing her temple as he gently gathered her in his arms, "they seem to be accepting the notion of us as a couple again."

I'm the only one who isn't.

Liz drew a deep breath. "Which is not as it should be," she said, splaying her hands across his chest to wedge a distance between them.

His eyes became shuttered. "It isn't?"

He looked as if he wanted to kiss her. She knew if that happened, they would end up near his bed. And if they were near it, they would soon be in it. Naked. Liz prayed for strength. She looked Travis straight in the eye and in her firmest, most professional tone said, "Your legal situation has to take precedence over all else right now. At least until after the depositions on Saturday."

Travis recoiled as if a bucket of cold water had been thrown over him. "You're right. Of course."

Feeling bereft that he hadn't said to hell with the consequences and kissed her anyway—at least once—she lifted the laptop she'd brought over with her and set it on the table. "So let's get down to it."

Two hours later, they sat staring at all the emails and restaurant receipts they had compiled.

Travis picked up the closest thing they had to a smoking gun and swore. He read the email in his hand, dated two days before Olympia had signed on as his client at Haverty, Brockman & Roberts. He had written, I still think full disclosure is the way to go.

Liz picked up another, from Olympia and read, "It's really not necessary at this point and may never be."

Travis sat back in disgust and muttered, "And we both know that can be interpreted any number of ways."

Liz couldn't argue with that. "You never prepared a sample document that would have disclosed your relationship with her? Just for her to look at?" *Please tell me you did.*

He shook his head grimly. "There was no point."

Liz stayed strong and focused on the positive. "At least we have, through the restaurant receipts, text messages and various emails, confirmation of your social engagements with her and the exact dates of your relationship. That's a start. And we have the wildcatter's testimony that you did everything you could to persuade him, to the point you were a major nuisance to him."

Travis raked his hands through his hair, then he stood and began to pace. "That could be used against me, too. Olympia could assert that it was my overzealousness that caused her to lose the deal."

"Overzealousness prompted by her emails," Liz corrected, trying not to notice how handsome and sexy Travis looked in the muted light of the cabin. "We have proof of how hard she was pushing you to close a deal with Dobbs."

"True," Travis allowed brusquely. "But we're going to need more," he continued, a brooding looking on his face.

"And we'll find it," Liz promised firmly.

"How?"

The sound of the dogs' fierce barking had him abruptly leaving his seat. Liz was right after him. By the time they reached the porch, the two mutts were racing toward the barn, where quite a ruckus of bleating and baaing was going on.

Liz and Travis gave chase, too. "I hope a predator hasn't found its way in with the goats!" she panted.

As it turned out, that wasn't the case.

The twelve goats were gathered in the barn, with two in the center butting, shoving and biting. The others were watching, sometimes pushing forward, sometimes stumbling to get out of the way. The dogs were still barking, adding to the commotion, though the two battling angoras paid no attention to them.

Travis stared. "What the…?" He whistled at his dogs and they swung toward him immediately. He pointed authoritatively toward the door. "Sit."

They both complied.

Meanwhile, the drama with the goats continued, as

Buck, the lone male in the group, fought off Queenie, the biggest female in the bunch.

The bleating and baaing escalated, until the buck went end over end.

The female stood triumphant.

All commotion stopped. The buck got up and, seemingly unhurt, wandered off as if nothing had happened. The rest of the herd dispersed, many of them going over to get a drink of water. Others went to lie down.

Liz scanned the flock, then headed for one goat in the corner and knelt down next to it. "I think this one might be sick."

"TRANSPORT STRESS," veterinarian Kurt McCabe said half an hour later, after he had finished examining the lethargic gray goat.

He put his stethescope and thermometer away.

"Fortunately, there's no sign of pneumonia or shipping fever yet. But she is dehydrated, so I recommend giving her water spiked with molasses, goat Nutri-Drench and some probiotics, just to be on the safe side."

"Should we separate her from the herd?" Travis asked.

Liz knelt down to pet the ailing animal. Although they hadn't had goats since she was in elementary school, she remembered a lot about caring for them. As well as how docile they usually were. "That would only increase her anxiety," she said.

Kurt snapped the latch on his bag and nodded in agreement. He looked at the other eleven goats, which were alternately roaming the barn and huddling in the aisle. "Best to keep them all together while they adjust to their new surroundings."

"What about the fighting?" Travis asked in concern, keeping an eye out for the largest female, who still seemed ready to rumble. Luckily, Liz noted, none of the other goats wanted to get rowdy with Queenie.

"It should settle down in a couple days, once they establish the hierarchy of the herd," Kurt said.

"That happens whenever you get a new group of goats together, or diminish an existing herd," Liz explained.

"Right again," Kurt said warmly. He turned to Travis and slapped a companionable hand on his old school chum's shoulder. "Got to say, Anderson. Never expected you to be herding goats."

Nor had Travis, Liz thought, catching his grimace.

Of course, if Travis hadn't made a mistake with a client, he wouldn't be back in Laramie County, never mind here bartering ranch work for legal services.

Liz fell into step beside the two men as they left the barn. "Given a choice, I am sure he wouldn't be," she felt obliged to say in defense.

Another mistake. Travis didn't seem to appreciate her aid.

Kurt narrowed his eyes. "Are you two…an item again?"

Liz flushed. So much for privacy. "What makes you think that?" she asked, damning herself for having given her feelings away.

He shrugged. "Body language. The way you're looking at each other." He reached his truck. "An air of intimacy or solidarity between the two of you. Take your pick."

Suddenly all possessive male, Travis smiled, clamped a hand on Liz's shoulder and pulled her to his side. Proudly, he told their old friend, "We're back on again."

He paused to playfully ruffle her hair and kiss her brow. "My only regret is that it ever ended."

"DID YOU HAVE TO TELL Kurt that?" Liz demanded irritably when the vet had left, and she and Travis headed for the kitchen to get some molasses. "Now it will be all over town."

He watched her mix up a bucket of water and several tablespoons of concentrated sugar. "I'm not going to pretend I'm not interested in you."

Liz went to rinse some sticky dark brown sugar off her finger. "The case—"

"Is about me not being one hundred percent truthful about my relationship with a woman." Travis joined her at the sink. He stood with his back to the faucet, hips against the counter, brawny arms crossed in front of him.

She tipped up her head and met his gaze, seeing both the heat and the tension there, and her stomach quivered.

"Had I not agreed to hide my involvement with Olympia before she signed on as a client, at least half this mess I am in would be a nonissue."

"It's not the same," Liz argued, her voice far too unsteady to convince herself, never mind him.

He slid an arm around her and pulled her close, brushing his lips across her temple. "It's exactly the same." He dipped his head and lightly pressed his mouth to hers.

Liz moaned in dismay. "You make it impossible for me to think when you do that." But she didn't step back. Not yet anyway…

He tugged her even nearer, leaning his body into hers. "Actually, I believe it's the other way around," he murmured. "I think when we're *kissing*—" he emphasized the word with a quick, breath-stealing caress "—is the only time either of us think clearly."

Without warning, Tillie appeared in the kitchen doorway. She was followed by other family members. "There you are! What did the vet say?"

Briefly, Travis caught the ladies and J.T.—who was still there, playing cards with them—up on the latest with the goats.

"I'm about to take the molasses water out to the sick goat now," Liz said.

"Before you go…" Tillie rushed out of the kitchen and returned with a FedEx envelope. "I'm so sorry, Travis," she said, her cheeks pink with embarrassment. "I've been so busy this completely slipped my mind. This came for you earlier today."

"Thanks." He looked at the return address. Liz could see it, too. It was from the human resources department at Anderson Oil. His grandfather's company…

"Do you-all want to play cards with us when you finish in the barn?" Reba asked.

Liz lifted a hand. "Thanks, Mom, but we still have some strategizing to do."

Her announcement was met with a quartet of speculative looks. Feeling as if she had been under the microscope long enough, she picked up the pitcher of molasses water. "Let's get going…."

Travis tipped his hat at J.T. and the ladies and ambled out after her.

Once on the porch, Liz paused as he opened the envelope. The look on his face was not promising.

Liz set the bucket down. "I hope it's good news."

Travis looked at her. "Depends on who's doing the deciding."

Her heart went out to him and she moved closer, glancing at the open V of his shirt and the strong column of his throat. "Feel like sharing?"

Travis gave her a thoughtful once-over. Wordlessly, he handed her the top sheet of the stack of papers.

Liz scanned the letter from human resources. "Wow," she said. "Seven figures plus a signing bonus and the title of vice president." She swallowed around the sudden constriction in her throat. "Your grandfather is pulling out all the stops."

"Don't forget the corner office on the top floor of the Anderson Oil building in downtown Houston," he responded drolly.

An office that would take him far away from her, Laramie County and the Four Winds Ranch. But wasn't that the goal here? Forgetting that would lead to nothing but heartbreak, and Liz had suffered enough heartbreak at the hands of Travis Anderson.

She picked up the bucket again and headed across the yard. Travis fell into step beside her even as she forced herself to conclude practically, "It's a great offer."

He reached over and took the bucket from her, easily carrying with one hand what it had taken her two to tote.

"If that was what I wanted to do," he agreed, his warm breath brushing her ear. "It isn't."

Silence fell as they continued to the barn. Trying not to think about what the future held—it was enough just to get through the present—Liz grew pensive as they went inside. Travis mixed probiotic powder into goat feed and filled a syringe with Nutri-Drench, an electrolyte, vitamin and mineral concoction.

Together, they found the ailing goat curled up in the corner where they had left her. Liz held her jaw while

Travis emptied the syringe. When the goat had swallowed, they offered the feed, and filled a small water bowl with the molasses and water mixture. They stayed by her side until they got her to drink and eat. Satisfied she was doing okay, the two of them then offered the rest of the goats the same additional nutrition, as a precaution.

When all had finished, Travis and Liz locked up the barn for the night, and headed back toward the homestead, to continue preparing for the deposition.

"What are you thinking?" Travis asked later, when they took a much-needed break.

"That doing ranch work for hours on end after putting in a full day, and still having a lot of legal work to finish up really wears a gal down. And," Liz continued, refusing to admit what was really bothering her—the fact that Travis might leave a lot sooner than she had realized, "I also think the position your grandfather has offered you is one fine backup."

Liz stifled the mixture of sadness and defeat welling up within her. She thrust her hands in the pockets of her jeans and stubbornly pushed on, forcing herself to be practical. "If all else fails, and given where we are with your legal situation, it just might—"

Travis caught her arms and, pulling her hands from her pockets in the process, turned her to face him.

Her heart racing, Liz looked deep into his eyes. "I'd understand if you wanted to take the job."

"I don't want you to understand," Travis said gruffly, gathering her into his arms for a brief, searing kiss. He ran his fingers through her hair, kissed the sensitive spot on her neck. "I don't want you to want me to leave."

Liz drew a shaky breath. "I don't!" Desperate to protect her heart, to keep from harboring false hope, she pushed him back. "But I'm also a realist, Travis. And common sense says…" Her voice trailed off. She shook her head, afraid if she said anything more she would burst into tears.

Travis pressed a finger to her lips and finished the sentence for her. "Common sense says…that we keep fighting for what we want, when we want it, until we get it."

Liz couldn't help but agree with that.

Unfortunately, she had the feeling that when the dust settled, and his legal troubles were over, they would still be talking about two distinctly different things.

Chapter Twelve

"Why the glum face?" J.T. asked Liz late the next afternoon, when he walked into her office.

"I can't find the pattern of behavior I'm looking for on a case." And without it, she saw no way she could win....

"And yet," he guessed, "you know it's got to be there."

She nodded. "Once a person starts wanting, or feels entitled to, special treatment, it's an attitude that usually stays."

J.T. flashed a wan smile. "Are we talking about someone else now—like my tropical-lagoon-style swimming pool?"

"Yours is a special case, J.T. We all know that. Which is why we've all been working so hard to come up with a solution." Liz ushered him to a seat at the conference table, where plans were spread out for him to peruse.

J.T. studied them in silence. "This pool is awfully small."

"But it fits in the backyard. You can easily put up a privacy fence, for safety's sake. And best of all, it's a design the zoning and planning commission has agreed to approve immediately, so construction on it could begin right away."

J.T. continued to survey the plans, along with the sketches and photos the landscaping company subcontracting on the job had supplied.

"It would be a good compromise," she continued.

He rubbed his jaw. "I'm going to need to think about it for a few days."

Liz smiled in encouragement. "While you're doing that, please promise me—no more picketing or threatening to get out there yourself with a shovel."

"I promise. May I take these with me?"

"Absolutely." Liz walked J.T. out. "How did the guard donkey shopping go today?"

"Not well. The ones we found weren't all they were advertised to be, so your mom passed and decided to keep searching."

Liz groaned. "Oh, dear. That means we're going to have to coop the goats up in the barn again tonight."

"Guess they were pretty noisy last night."

"An understatement and a half," Liz murmured drily.

Queenie and Buck were jockeying for dominance, which in turn riled up all the other animals. Travis hadn't been happy. Nor had anyone else. No one had slept well. All she had been able to think about when she awoke was Travis, and how much she wanted to help him, and how much she wished she was still in his arms....

But common sense—and the need for privacy—had kept her firmly in her own bed in the ranch house, while he bunked down at the homestead.

As a consequence, it had been a long, lonely night. Fraught with fantasy and regret, worry and hope.

"Well, maybe it will be better tonight," J.T. said optimistically.

"I'll find out later." Liz squared her shoulders. "Right now, I've got another client coming in…."

"Good luck with that. I'll be in touch." J.T. took off, looking happier and more relaxed than she had seen him since his wife died.

Fifteen minutes later, the outer door to her office opened again and Travis walked in, with his expensive leather briefcase slung over one shoulder. He was dressed in a tan twill shirt, snug-fitting jeans and boots suitable for ranch work, but he looked like a lawyer striding into court. Strategically ready. Sexy. Confident. And determined to win.

Getting an idea what he must be like in negotiations, Liz watched him take out several fat files. "You've been busy," she said admiringly.

"I organized copies of all the correspondence I wrote on Olympia's behalf, just as you asked."

"Good."

He handed her another folder, his callused fingers brushing her slightly in the transfer. "The receipts for dinners and lunches out, in chronological order."

There were so many of them. The affair must have been intense. Liz pushed the twinge of jealousy away. She had no room for that. No room for emotion of any kind. "Also good," she said in the most casual voice she could manage.

Travis opened a third folder. "Copies of all the text messages we sent, confirming the various engagements and business dealings. Also arranged in the order they were sent." He held out a fourth. "And all my meeting notes, along with memos summarizing any other discussions we had during the course of my representation of her."

Liz perused a few of them, noting the attention to

detail. Which didn't surprise her. Travis excelled at everything he did.

In and out of bed…

She swallowed, pushing the thought away.

He sat on the edge of her desk, facing her. Something hot and sensual shimmered in his eyes. "How are things going on your end? Were you able to speak with any of Olympia's four previous attorneys?"

"Yes, I did. By phone."

"And?" He lifted a brow.

Reluctantly, Liz admitted, "The first two were not asked for a reduction in billing rate. The third and fourth both were, but elected not to give it to her, since it was not their firm's policy."

Travis went still. "What about a relationship?"

"If it happened, no one is admitting it," Liz said with a sigh.

His lips compressed. "So this pattern of behavior began and ended with me."

"As far as we know. I mean, we can ask during the course of the deposition if she is still receiving a reduced billing rate from Haverty, Brockman & Roberts. And whether or not she's dating anyone else in the firm."

"My guess is yes to the first and no to the second, given what happened to me."

Liz nodded.

A dejected silence fell.

Travis stood and moved away from the desk. "So, the deposition is in two days. And we're back to 'he said, she said.'"

Liz rose and followed him to the shelves containing her law books. "You still have a solid case for unlawful firing and defamation."

"Part of my job was keeping the client happy." His jaw clenched. "HB&R can and will argue I failed to do that."

Liz refused to admit defeat. "And we'll argue in return that no attorney can keep Olympia Herndon happy for long. Her track record when it comes to representation speaks for itself, and I am ready and willing to call in her previous attorneys and ask them under oath exactly how demanding and difficult a client she was."

"That will get ugly."

Liz knew he was thinking about his family, trying to keep them from being involved—by extension—in anything undignified or defamatory. But while she sympathized with that, her job was to protect him.

"It's already ugly. We just have to hope that, when it comes right down to it, everyone involved will realize this is a can't-win situation, with the potential to hurt all the participants."

"It sounds like you're talking settlement already." Lines of disapproval bracketed his lips.

"No. I'm talking about a voluntary withdrawal of all charges, with binding confidentiality agreements on both sides. A win-win solution for all of us that will keep the ugliness confined to the deposition room and out of the public eye. It's quite a different animal." Liz paused. "Trust me to petition well on your behalf."

"I do." Travis took her hand and squeezed it. They smiled at each other, in sync once again. "In the meantime, I have a favor to ask of you…"

"DINNER WITH YOUR FOLKS, at their ranch," Liz repeated in shock. "Tonight." They hadn't even done that when they were dating.

Travis glanced at his watch. "We're due there as we speak."

"I'm in a suit." Or in other words, way overdressed, so at a disadvantage, socially and otherwise.

Travis lounged against the wall and surveyed her head to toe. "You could be wearing Birkenstocks and a toga, with a wreath in your hair, for all they'd care."

Liz went to the wardrobe and supply closet in her office, where she kept a few emergency outfits. She opened it, and stood looking at the choices.

Travis hovered next to her. "I wouldn't ask you if I didn't really want you by my side tonight."

Her heart took a little leap. "Put that way...of course I'll go." She removed a white, notch-collared blouse and black slacks. That and her black flats were the best she could do.

She slipped into her private bathroom and shut the door.

Travis called through the panel, "I've already told them we can't stay past dinner, so it shouldn't be a long evening."

Liz hurriedly changed clothes. "Any of your siblings going to be there?" He had two sisters and two brothers. All younger.

"Nope. I'm not sure whether to be happy about that or sad."

She ran a brush through her hair, reapplied lipstick and spritzed on a small amount of jasmine perfume, then opened the bathroom door. "How come?"

Travis lifted one corner of his mouth as she approached him. "If they were there," he admitted with uncharacteristic ruefulness, "they'd take some of the attention away from me."

Liz shut down her computer, picked up her handbag

and keys and turned off the lights. She led the way out. "So you think this is going to be a tense situation?"

Travis fell into step beside her. "Hopefully not, with you there."

The excitement Liz'd felt began to fade.

So much for presuming this invitation was romantic in nature.

She paused and turned to face him, so suddenly he almost ran into her. "In other words, you're using me as a human shield?" She kept her voice mild.

He curved his hands over her shoulders, his eyes full of affection. "More like the target of my longing." He rubbed his thumb across her cheek.

Liz sighed and tried not to lean into his touch. "You think sweet-talking me will you get somewhere?"

He flashed a slow, sexy grin. "One can hope." Then he bent his head and kissed her. "I'll make this up to you," he promised.

He was going to have to, Liz thought. Her emotions were in such turmoil!

Talk once again turned to his legal situation and the strategy they were planning to take.

Twenty minutes later, they arrived at Travis's parents' ranch.

Located on the northeastern side of Laramie County, the former Lockhart Ranch had belonged to Kelsey's family, until Kelsey Lockhart and Brady Anderson had partnered up to purchase the property and renamed it the Double Deal Ranch.

Over much familial protesting, Travis's parents had entered into a marriage of convenience—that soon turned into the real thing—in order to get a start-up loan for their two businesses. Thirty-four years and five children later, Kelsey and Brady were happy and prosperous.

Kelsey's horse-riding operation took up one half of the ranch, Brady's cattle operation the rest. They employed a half-dozen riding instructors, a dozen full-time cowboys and a dozen grooms, a cook and two secretaries. Everything on the ranch was modern, luxurious and state-of-the-art. Including their very own backyard barbecue pavilion. The spacious entertaining area featured a beautiful limestone floor, polished oak bar and stools, and banquet table. A mammoth grill and Sub-Zero fridge, plus sink and dishwasher, comprised the outdoor kitchen area. Flat-screen TVs and ceiling fans were suspended from the roof.

Liz recalled being intimidated the one time she had come out here to meet his parents, when she was a teenager and dating Travis. They had stayed only a few minutes, but it had still been nerve-racking.

That was nothing compared to the way she felt now, as she and Travis walked across the patio toward his waiting parents.

Brady was behind the polished oak bar, making margaritas. Kelsey was setting a bouquet of flowers on the table. The scents of mesquite-smoked chicken and baking bread filled the air.

The evening was all set to be homey and welcoming, yet she felt as if she was under scrutiny, however polite.

That feeling intensified when they sat down to dinner.

During the meal, the conversation was light and casual. It was only when they were finishing up with pie and coffee that Travis's parents finally exchanged glances and got down to brass tacks. "Hargett told us about his offer to you," Kelsey told her son, her freckles standing out against her fair skin.

"Before you decide, your mother and I would like to put in our own offer," Brady said.

Liz's discomfort intensified. "Perhaps I shouldn't be here for this…" She started to rise.

Travis draped a possessive arm around her shoulders and used the pressure to push her right back down in her seat.

He turned to face her, stating simply, "I want you with me."

The sensation of being needed made her spirits soar.

He regarded his parents steadily. "Liz can hear anything you-all have to say to me this evening."

Brady wasn't happy about it, but he nodded and continued with the frankness for which he and his wife were known. "Son, if you want to ranch, we want you to start out right. Not to insult you, Liz, but we don't want to see our son herding goats and donkeys on someone else's property when he could be running cattle on his own. Which is why, Travis, your mother and I are prepared to lease you a chunk of our land to get started on. When and if you find a ranch you'd like to buy, we'll help you with that, too."

Clearly insulted, Travis removed his arm from Liz's shoulders and sat up straight. "I appreciate the offer, but…no."

A tense silence fell.

Finally, Kelsey bit her lip. "We just want you to know there are options."

"My name will be cleared," Travis stated firmly.

The Andersons cast hesitant looks at Liz.

Suddenly, she knew where this was going. Anxiety choked her throat. "You're concerned that Travis asked me to represent him, instead of going with a big and powerful Houston law firm," she said hoarsely. And having already said as much to him, to no avail, they were now prepared to appeal to her.

Sagely, Brady commented, "It would seem that path would level the playing field a lot more than the one he is on now."

Kelsey leaned toward her oldest son. "You've worked so hard for so long to get where you are in your law career. We don't want to see you pushed off the fast track and forced to give up all that hard-won success."

Awash with hurt and embarrassment, Liz interjected, "I don't want that, either. And if it would make you feel better, I will recuse myself from this situation." *If for no other reason than to regain my dignity.*

Travis scowled and nudged her leg under the table. "No, you won't!" he countered.

Heat flowed through her. Liz moved her leg back so they were no longer touching. "Travis..."

A muscle worked in his jaw as he captured her hand and held tight. "Mom. Dad. I'm sorry this situation has embarrassed you. It's humiliated the heck out of me, too." He leaned forward penitently. "It's also my fault. I used poor judgment. Instead of holding out for something better—something like you and Dad have—I got involved in a casual relationship that I knew from the outset was destined to end. Possibly even badly..." He huffed in frustration, his gaze direct. "Well, it has. Not for the reasons I would have assumed, but still in a way that's created havoc in my life."

Brady's scowl deepened. He started to speak.

Travis cut him off. "Liz is doing a fine job representing me." He rubbed his thumb over the back of her wrist. "I have faith in her. And if you respect me at all…" he paused to let his words sink in "…you'll accept my judgment on this and trust her, too."

Maternal worry clouded Kelsey's eyes as she got up to pour them all more coffee. "Have you thought about what an uncomfortable position Liz is now in?" she demanded, glaring at her son.

"It was one thing when the two of you were little more than old acquaintances. But now…" When his mother sat down again, her expression turned pleading. "Travis, if this doesn't go well, it can and will affect your relationship."

Just as his single-minded ambition once had.

"Your parents are right." Liz wrenched her hand from Travis's and struggled to her feet.

Much as she was loath to admit it, his parents weren't blowing hot air.

Travis had been playing cowboy and living on the Four Winds as a way of escaping. But soon the depositions would bring them sharply back to reality.

And the truth was, Travis belonged in a big, fancy law office, in the heart of Houston, along with all the other power players.

She might be content to live in a small town, helping those around her with problems large and small. Travis never would be. Not in the long term, anyway.

Liz inhaled a shuddering breath. "Since I've been representing you, the situation has gotten even more perilous and complex."

Travis's head lifted in surprise.

"Olympia is determined to make you pay for being unable to get her the business deal she wanted." To the point the oil heiress appeared ready to do and say anything.

Travis pushed his empty dessert plate away and downed the rest of his coffee. "The truth is on our side."

Unfortunately, Liz knew, truth did not always prevail in court.

"Hargett is acquainted with her family. He says Olympia can be vicious when crossed," Kelsey interjected. "He's worried you aren't as prepared as you should be."

Liz knew they weren't even close. What if her emotions got in the way of the defense she was crafting? What if she screwed up?

Kelsey went on, "All your father and I are saying, Travis, is that if there is something between you and Liz—and it seems that there is—why risk that?"

"Why not let someone else handle your defense?" Brady said.

So that if the attempt to prove the accusations false failed, someone else would take the blame, Liz thought. She and Travis could go on....

"Look," Travis said, standing in turn. He glared at his parents. "Just because you love me does not give you the right to try to run my life."

"That's not what we're doing," Kelsey protested, visibly upset.

"Really?" he countered, circling around the table to take Liz's hand. Clasping her fingers tightly, he drew her out from beneath the pavilion. "Because it sure as heck seems like it is!"

"I'm sorry," Liz said miserably when they reached the driveway.

He reached the passenger door, suddenly growing very quiet, very serious. "Don't be. This has nothing to do with you."

She stared at him, her stomach twisting with a combination of tension and nerves.

"It's always been like this," Travis continued in frustration. He lounged against the side of the truck, arms folded in front of him.

In a low, furious voice he confided, "Because I'm the oldest, I've always been expected to be perfect, to live up to the image my parents have of me in their heads. I'm expected to set an example, Liz. And I have. All the way through high school and college and law school, I was damn near perfect."

"Yeah, you were," Liz recalled in open admiration. So much that she'd been left feeling not just too young for him, but unworthy....

He dipped his head in acknowledgment of her compliment, all the while holding her gaze.

"Editor of *Texas Law Review,* top in my class. Really good job with a big firm. I was on the fast track to huge success." His lips curved ruefully, in a way that did funny things to her insides.

"And then I screwed up." He shrugged his shoulders. "And my parents can't accept it."

She edged closer, her arms folded, too. "I think they're just worried about you," she murmured compassionately.

As am I.

He reached out and pried her hand loose, covering them with his. His usual confidence was back. "I'll be all right, Liz...no matter what happens." His fingers tightened. "I've got the job on the Four Winds and a place to live."

Which was so much less than what he was meant for, she realized sadly.

She drew a breath, lifted her chin. "You've also got the offer from your grandfather."

Which would ensure a seven-figure salary and a lot of power and prestige.

"And the offer from your parents." If being a rancher was truly what he wanted. And Liz wasn't sure it was.

Clenching his jaw, he opened the passenger door. "I'm not taking either of those."

Liz delayed climbing inside the cab. Emotions rioting, she gripped the armrest. "Why not?"

Travis wrapped his hands around her waist and lifted her into the seat, the same way he'd lifted her against the wall when he'd made love with her.

"Because there is no dignity in nepotism." He let her go, stepped away. "I'm not falling back on the family coffers. I've got too much self-respect for that." He leaned inside the cab, cupped her face in his palm. "I want to live my own life, my own way."

He pressed his lips to hers and kissed her on the mouth, in full view of the Double Deal ranch house and anyone who might be passing.

Liz clutched at his shirt. He kissed her again.

"Starting now," he promised in a husky voice.

Her heart pounding, Liz flattened her palms on his chest. "Travis," she moaned. If he didn't stop…

He tangled his tongue with hers, dragging his fingers through her hair. "Let's go somewhere we can be alone. A hotel in San Angelo, maybe…"

How Liz wished they could forget everything and just go off somewhere, close out the world and make love. Over and over again.

But the lawyer in her knew it would be a very bad path to take.

Ignoring the weightless feeling in her tummy and the ache between her thighs, she shook her head and straightened. "No, Travis. I have work to do. And so do you."

Chapter Thirteen

Liz walked into the Four Winds kitchen a little past eight o'clock, her thoughts still focused on the recent talk with Travis and his parents. Although they hadn't come right out and said so, their concern made her wonder whether she was helping Travis get his life back, or merely standing in the way of his inevitable departure. One thing was sure: she did not have a documented pattern of behavior that would hold up in court and prove Olympia Herndon had set out to use—and possibly destroy—Travis's career, for the oil heiress's own gain.

Her emotions in turmoil, Liz looked at Faye Elizabeth, who was reading through a stack of what appeared to be business papers at the kitchen table.

Aware that it was past time for her to do her own ranch chores, Liz said, "Just let me change clothes and I'll go out and bring the goats in."

Her grandmother sipped her tea. "Not necessary. Reba and J.T. have already put them in the barn."

Surprise rendered Liz momentarily speechless. "J.T. is here? Again?" The irascible widower was certainly getting out more. In what appeared to be a good way this time.

Faye Elizabeth nodded. "He and your mother went

for a walk. He has some important decisions to make and he wanted her opinion."

Liz focused on the two sets of plates and silverware next to the stove. Regret mixed with guilt as she realized yet another mistake on her part.

Faye Elizabeth rose. "Sit down. I'll fix your plate."

"I'm so sorry, Grandma…I already ate," she said sheepishly. "So did Travis. His parents invited us to their ranch at the last second, I forgot to tell you."

Waving off the error, Faye Elizabeth grabbed a potholder and lifted a cast-iron skillet out of the oven. In it were two chicken-fried steaks, crisp and golden-brown. In a smaller one was cream gravy. A third held two generous helpings of mashed potatoes on one side, green beans on the other. "No problem." She began putting the food in airtight containers. "We'll have it for lunch tomorrow. It'll save me from cooking then."

Liz set her briefcase down on a chair. Springing into action, she grabbed a white chef's apron from the hook in the pantry. "At least let me help with the dishes…."

Liz carried the three empty skillets to the farmhouse-style sink and set them down. Out the window, she could see Travis striding toward the dogs, who were running to greet him.

He knelt down as he reached them, and both, tails wagging, bounded into his arms, licking him under the chin.

A wide grin split his handsome face. He ruffled their fur, massaging them with his palm.

Knowing all too well the magic of his touch, and the impact it had on her, Liz sighed.

Damn, but she had gotten used to seeing him every day. At breakfast and dinner. In the barn. On horseback.

In his bed…

Hair rumpled, muscles taut. His eyes telling her that he wanted her and only her. Right then, right there…

Liz inhaled a jerky breath.

Trying not to think about what life would be like on the Four Winds without him, she picked up a bottle of dish soap and squirted a generous portion on the bottom of each pan, then began running the water.

Faye Elizabeth appeared at her elbow, drawing Liz's attention away from the window and the man striding off toward the corral, dogs in tow. She peered into Liz's face. "That must have been one stressful get-together at the Double Deal," she remarked sagely.

Liz really didn't want to talk about it. She picked up the nylon scrubber sponge and went to work on the crustiest skillet, rubbing with all her might.

She had to stop thinking about making love with Travis. And wishing she could be beneath the sheets with him right now.

"What makes you say that?" She shifted and forced herself to ignore the fluttering in her middle.

"You just put soap and water in three of my favorite cast-iron pans."

Liz gasped and slapped a sudsy hand against her chest. She muttered a silent curse. "I wasn't supposed to get them wet." She cringed and slanted a look at the family's premiere cook. These pots and pans were as precious as gold to the accomplished chef. "Was I…?"

Faye Elizabeth shook her head. "You clean them with salt and paper towels, and then rub them down with oil."

Feeling more inept than ever on the home front, Liz dumped out the water. Simply washed and dried and left that way, the pans would rust. "I'll dry them off, clean them correctly and reseason them in the oven," she volunteered.

Faye Elizabeth pulled her away from the sink. "I can do that later." She peered at Liz in concern. "You need to take a deep breath and tell me what's going on that has you so flustered."

Her grandmother guided Liz through the mudroom and out onto the back porch.

Liz sat down and turned her glance away from the sight of Travis putting out feed for the horses. Being careful not to violate client confidentiality, she explained the Andersons' concern. "And they're right, because if Travis had taken money from his family and hired a big-name attorney from a big Texas firm to defend him, he'd have a lot more resources at his disposal right now." Liz sighed and dropped her head in her hands. "Maybe I have taken on more than I can handle. And I'm being out-lawyered even as we speak."

Her grandma patted her on the back. "It's not like you to be so down on yourself. Usually you thrive on working to help the underdogs in any situation. You're so confident and focused on the law."

Liz knew that, too. Which meant her personal ties to Travis were getting in the way of her ability to do her job.

She cast another glance at Travis. Looking every inch a Texas cowboy, instead of a city lawyer, he was pumping water into the troughs.

Liz turned back to her grandmother and sighed in frustration. "Travis's whole future is at stake." As, in a way, was hers.

Faye Elizabeth frowned. "Your clients' futures are always at stake. That's why they come to you in the first place." She searched Liz's face. "What's different this time?"

What indeed?

"Unless…" her jaw dropped "…you're falling in love with him?"

Liz looked into her grandmother's eyes. The usual disapproval and wariness were curiously missing. Instead, Liz saw only tenderness.

"*Are* you falling in love with him?" Faye Elizabeth pressed.

Was she? Liz wrinkled her nose. "I thought you disapproved of me seeing him."

Faye Elizabeth snorted. "I'm always wary of you getting hurt."

"Then…?"

"Let's just say he's been so persistent in his pursuit of you, he's beginning to grow on me." She sized Liz up. "And, by the way, you didn't answer my question."

Liz flushed and resisted the urge to glance again at the only man she had ever cared about so deeply. "Because I don't know how to answer it." *I don't know how I feel. And right now, with the deposition looming, I'm not sure I want to know.*

The door to the porch opened, and Reba and J.T. walked out of the house. Saved by another member of the family, Liz thought, in relief. She vaulted to her feet. "Hi, you two." She noted that they both looked happier than she had seen them in a while.

Plus her mom was not moving nearly as stiffly as before, which must mean her sciatica was abating.

Reba sat down on the edge of a white wicker chair. "Did you see the contracts on the kitchen table from Hill Country Donkeys?"

The ones Faye Elizabeth had been reviewing? "I did," Liz said with a nod.

Reba continued soberly, "I was out there earlier today, looking at a couple of donkeys. But there are a few clauses in the contract that I think might be deal-breakers, so—"

She stopped in midsentence as out in the barn a ruckus of baas and bleats rent the air, and all hell broke loose.

TRAVIS AND THE DOGS RACED to the barn. He got there ahead of Liz, but just barely. Reba, J.T. and Faye Elizabeth were fast on her heels. He slid open the heavy doors and let the two dogs inside.

In the middle of the barn, a rumble was going on.

All twelve goats seemed to be involved in some way. Whether hiding along the edges, as two of the smaller ones were, or pressing in between the largest female and only male—aka Queenie and Buck—they were baaing and bleating, kicking and butting.

The dogs ran around the edges, barking at them to stop. For all the damn good it did, Travis noted in frustration.

Queenie went after Buck with all her might, shoving him against the wall. When that failed to make him back down, she rammed her horns into his side. Her opponent recoiled, bleating loudly. Blood ran down his side.

Liz shouted in distress, "Travis! Buck's hurt!"

"I see that!" he yelled back. Grimacing, he waded through the flock, shoving goats aside until he got to Queenie. Head down, she was going after Buck once again, so Travis quickly grabbed her, one hand around her middle, the other behind her neck so she couldn't spear him with her horns. Ignoring her furious response, he lifted her off her feet and carried her to a birthing stall at the far end of the building, pushed her inside and firmly closed the heavy wooden door.

Pounding ensued as the goat kicked and butted, trying to get out.

The other animals scattered.

J.T., Faye Elizabeth and Reba enlisted the help of the still-barking dogs and herded the rest of the goats outside to the fenced pasture closest to the barn. Only Buck remained.

Speaking soothingly, Liz approached him.

The billy goat stared at her, bleating softly, blood dripping down his side. Liz sighed and shook her head. "He's going to need stitches."

Travis's mood was as grim as he moved in to assist. "I'll help you get him to the vet."

To Liz's RELIEF, Kurt McCabe met them at his office in town. The vaunted local vet sedated the injured animal and asked them about what had happened while he cleaned and stitched up the wound.

Relaxing in Travis's steady, calm presence, Liz told their old school pal the whole story. "Thank heaven Travis was there to help out. None of us would have been strong enough to intervene in the fight. He's really good in a crisis."

Kurt sent Travis a wry, sidelong look that seemed to ask, *And what have you been up to, buddy, besides romancing the local lady lawyer?* "Really?" he dead-panned.

Liz resisted the urge to sink through the floor. Aware she had just given too much away, she sucked in a breath and continued her tale. "Anyway, we haven't had goats on the property for a long time, but I don't recall anything like this ever happening before." Deciding she was standing too close to Travis, she paced restlessly to the other side of the room, ostensibly for a better view.

"Of course, I don't remember having any bucks on the property before. I think we just had females."

Travis chuckled. Once again, he and Kurt exchanged man-to-man grins.

"In keeping with the Four Winds tradition, I suppose?" Travis joked.

"What's the saying?" Liz countered in her best country drawl, returning his teasing glance. "Don't go fixin' what ain't broke to begin with?"

"Uh-oh, cowpoke. Sounds like you may not be bunking there for very much longer, after all," Kurt teased. "Too much testosterone for the Four Winds."

Travis frowned and looked at Liz, as if daring her to declare the same.

Aware she was beginning to depend on him more and more—maybe too much—she shrugged. "I'll have to ask my mom if you're why she dared bring a male into the herd this time. Although I have to say, it seems like Buck here was on the losing end of the battle with Queenie."

"Happens sometimes," Kurt said.

Travis and Liz looked at the vet, who finished stitching, then bandaged the wound. "Goats are hierarchical. Every herd has a dominant female and a head buck. They'll both fight for the top position among their gender, but they don't usually fight the opposite sex."

"Then why do you think she keeps going after him?" Liz asked.

Kurt shrugged. "Can't really say. Maybe she's a bully and entertains herself by pushing others around. Maybe she just likes to be dominant, or to fight and win."

He stripped off his gloves and stepped over to the sink to wash his hands. "Whatever the reason, you've got a problem here, because it may not be in her nature to behave any differently, no matter what herd she's in." Kurt paused. "She's two years old, so she's been around awhile. Does she have a history of this behavior?"

"I don't know." *If I had been pulling my weight, running the ranch, I would know the answer to this and many other questions,* Liz thought. Knowing she couldn't undo the past but only handle things more responsibly in the future, she added, "But I'll find out."

It was dark when Liz and Travis started back to the ranch, leaving the sedated billy goat at Kurt's office. En route, she got the number of the farm Queenie had come from and called them. She talked briefly to the owner.

"Well?" Travis said, as soon as she had finished. He sent her a curious glance.

Liz leaned back in her seat, liking the confident, careful way he drove. They had been thrown together a lot recently and there was no doubt he was nice company.

Liz rubbed at a spot of dried blood and mud on her jeans, from getting the injured goat bandaged and loaded in the hauler for transport. "Apparently, Queenie's been sold several times. But she's always had to be returned."

Travis picked up speed as they hit the open road. The headlight beams illuminated the dark countryside, while light from the dash filled the cab with an intimate glow. "That would have been nice to know beforehand."

"No kidding." Liz admired the firm line of his jaw, the sculpted shape of his lips. Though she wanted nothing more than to have him pull over and make out with her again, she kept the talk focused on business. "The breeders have agreed to take Queenie back and replace her with a more docile female."

Travis turned the pickup onto the ranch road and drove beneath the Four Winds sign toward the house. "Which means the fight for top spot will begin all over again."

"Um-hmm. The question is why does the process have to be so rough and ugly?"

He shrugged. "Why do a lot of things have to be rough and ugly?"

There was no answer, Liz knew. But her thoughts drifted, focusing again on what Kurt had said in reference to Queenie.

Maybe she's a bully and entertains herself by pushing others around. Maybe she just likes to be dominant. Or to fight and win. Whatever the reason, you've got a problem here, because it may not be in her nature to behave any differently....

And then it hit Liz like a lightning bolt. There was a pattern of behavior to be found that could win their case! She had just been looking in the wrong place....

When Travis cut the engine, she vaulted out of the truck, eager to get to work.

"What's going on?" he asked, circling around to join her.

Leery of speaking too soon and raising his hopes, only to dash them again, Liz only said, "I have a lot more to do to prepare for the deposition. So if you wouldn't mind...can we call it a night?"

"WHAT DO YOU MEAN, Liz is gone?" Travis asked early the next morning.

Tillie looked up from her breakfast. "She left last night, right after you got back from the vet. I assumed you knew."

He hadn't. But then, he'd been stuck at the homestead. Alone. "Did she say where she was going?" he asked casually as he walked over to pour himself a cup of coffee.

"Houston." Faye Elizabeth handed him a plate. "She had some things to do before the deposition on Saturday morning. She said she was going to meet up with you there. Is that not the plan?"

It was now. Irked, because it seemed as if his life was spiraling out of control again. Travis coolly played along.

"I'll be joining Liz in Houston this evening," he told the women as he poured maple syrup on his hotcakes. "First, however, I need to pick up Buck at the vet and then return Queenie to the goat farm where you-all got her—and select a replacement."

"What about the guard donkeys?" Faye Elizabeth set a large glass of milk in front of Travis.

"We can't purchase any until Liz has a chance to look at them," Reba said, "but not to worry. The goats'll be fine in the barn and pasture until Liz gets back."

The question was, would Travis be fine, if Liz kept shutting him out this way? He'd thought she was starting to let him near. Maybe not.

He forced himself to focus on the business at hand. "If you want, I can arrange for a hired hand from the Double Deal to fill in during our absence."

"That won't be necessary," Reba said. "We Cartwright women are used to handling things without a male presence. We do just fine without a man around."

"Maybe that should change," Faye Elizabeth interjected.

Everyone turned to look at her. "Are you talking about me or Liz?" Reba asked in a curt voice. "Because there's nothing but friendship between me and J.T. Nor will there ever be. I'm too independent and he's too in love with his late wife for that."

"She was talking about Liz," Tillie interjected. "And her future." She frowned at Reba. "And don't go spouting off about how all my great-granddaughter needs is a baby, not a man. Because a baby alone will never make our Lizzie happy. She needs the whole shebang." The wise matriarch turned to give Travis a long, contemplative look. "And I think we know just the man to give it to her...."

The Cartwright women were expecting a lot from him, Travis thought, as he headed out to get Queenie for her trip back to the goat farm. The funny thing was, he was beginning to want to give a lot, too.

He knew Liz was focused on the malpractice charges against him. That she wanted not only to avoid going to court, but to win.

He wanted that, too.

More than that, he wanted for it all to be over, so they could move forward. No longer be client and attorney— or ranch hand and reluctant lady rancher—but simply a man and woman destined to be together.

But in order to get there, he had to finish up his chores, see the Cartwright ladies were settled, and then head to Houston himself.

Unfortunately, nothing went as planned.

Queenie fought like hell, and he had a devil of a time getting her loaded up in the trailer.

The goat farm owners tried to give him another less than ideal animal in exchange for her, so he'd had to insist he look at all the females and go over their health and ownership histories.

Finally satisfied he had a good goat to take back to the ranch, Travis headed for town.

Buck was ready to go, but still groggy from the sedatives he'd been given the night before. The ride back to the ranch made him nauseated. What he did to the inside of the livestock hauler was not pretty, or fun to clean up.

Three more calves had been born, and Travis had to help Reba tend to them.

By then it was almost nightfall.

Worried how the women would fare in his absence, he ignored their protests and called over to the Double Deal, arranging for one hired hand to come during the day and another to be on standby at night.

After he phoned Liz to let her know he was on his way, he showered and packed, loaded his pickup and then headed for Houston.

It was nearly midnight by the time he arrived at the hotel where she had made reservations for both of them.

Instead of the warm welcome he expected, he found a message from Liz waiting for him at the front desk telling him she was still working hard gathering background information for the deposition, and instructing him to get a good night's sleep. She would meet him at the Starbucks across the street from the downtown offices of Haverty, Brockman & Roberts at 10:00 a.m. the next day.

Piqued that he hadn't received anything but the briefest of text messages since she had left, he carried his bags to his room. What the hell did any of this mean?

Was her prep going badly? Was she afraid to face him, because she thought they were going to lose? Had she discovered something that would exonerate him? And if so, why wasn't she telling him what it was?

And worst of all, why did he suddenly feel no more important to her than any other client?

Chapter Fourteen

Travis was at the Starbucks, sipping coffee and wondering if Liz was really going to show up, when the Town Car pulled up at the curb. The uniformed driver hopped out to get the door and Liz stepped out, looking gorgeous in a trim black suit and heels. Travis's heart dropped. He had missed her. And he was ticked off, too, about the way she had shut him out of whatever it was that had been going on with his case.

He understood why, of course. She was trying to keep a professional distance and focus on the deposition, which would be hard to do if she was lying wrapped in his arms. In his bed.

Still, it would have been nice to know where she'd been and what she'd been doing in the last thirty-six hours.

"Since when did you start riding around in a Town Car?" he asked, doing his best not to sound irked. The only person he knew who did that was his grandfather Hargett.

Liz bent her head, rummaging through her purse. She handed the driver a tip—which he refused.

Another clue that maybe the limo hadn't been her idea?

"The last few days," Liz murmured, distracted, putting the money back into her handbag. "It was just easier."

The driver smiled and got into the vehicle.

Resisting the primal urge to haul her into his arms and kiss her senseless, Travis slid his hands into the pockets of his suit pants. Liz was wearing understated gold jewelry, something else she never did. Her auburn hair looked pretty in the sunlight, even twisted into a sophisticated, all-business knot at the nape of her neck.

If he didn't know better, he would think she still lived and worked in the city.

And that made him wonder what possibilities there were for them, once his legal troubles were behind him.

Would they have unlimited options?

It depended on whatever tactics she had developed— without his knowledge.

Irritation tugged at him once again.

Focusing on the matter at hand, he asked, "Having a driver made it easier to do what?"

Liz waved at the chauffeur as he pulled away from the curb. "Get around town."

This had his grandfather's fingerprints all over it. "Doing…?" Travis prodded.

Liz did an about face and headed for the corner. She pressed the button at the crosswalk, then waited. "There's no time to go into it."

The light changed and they took off across the street. Travis leaned down to speak into her ear. "So you're not going to tell me what the game plan is. You just expect me to go into the deposition blind…."

Liz reached the other side and moved out of the way of other pedestrians. Standing against the building, she tipped up her head and, her emerald eyes serious, promised, "I'll explain everything later, in great detail. Right now it's better for both of us if we keep our emotions out of it."

Which meant what…she cared about him too much, or not at all?

No telling from the brisk, purposeful expression on her face.

More silence stretched between them.

She was waiting for his reaction. To see if he would give her the credit she wanted.

"I trust you," he said finally, realizing it was true. As much as he hated being left in the dark, he didn't think she would leave him hanging out to dry.

She kept her guard up. "Good," she said in a businesslike tone.

They walked into the building where he had once worked and took the elevator up to the twenty-sixth floor. Carol, at reception, started to smile, then stopped, uncertain, when she saw him.

Travis knew exactly how she felt.

He didn't know how to feel about being here again, except…confused. Part of him wanted the redemption he deserved. The other just wanted to get the hell away. Close this disappointing, tumultuous chapter of his life. And never look back.

Avoiding his eyes, the receptionist directed them where to go. Liz and Travis continued down the hall together. Knowing she had to keep in the game, Travis kept his distance. Liz had her head held high.

The firm partners and Olympia Herndon were waiting in the conference room, videotaping equipment and stenographer at the ready. Haverty, Brockman and Roberts all rose as Liz took her place at the table. Greetings were issued and returned, hands shaken.

"Shall we get down to it?" opposing counsel said.

Liz opened up her briefcase, her confidence apparent. "Absolutely."

"I want to be deposed first," Olympia announced.

In a white, silk wrap-dress and diamonds, her platinum-blond hair flowing loose around her shoulders, she looked like the pampered Southern heiress she was.

All eyes cut to Liz. She simply nodded in acquiescence, her expression giving nothing away.

Olympia sat back in her chair, crossing her legs at the knee. "Ask me anything you want about my affair with Travis Anderson." She drew a deep breath. "I'll be happy to tell you how Travis Anderson pressured me into sleeping with him. And then signing on with his firm, as his client." Her eyes glittered vindictively as she continued putting her talent for lying to use. "How after I broke up with him, he did everything he could to chase Digger Dobbs, the exceptionally talented wildcatter I was after, away."

"Actually, I'd prefer to start with your history with Herndon Oil," Liz said, looking down at the notes in front of her. Her attitude was as exacting—and professionally detached—as her tone. "How long have you been working for the family business?"

Olympia lifted a hand and fluffed the back of her hair. "Since I was fifteen."

"In an executive capacity," Liz clarified with an encouraging smile.

Her quarry shrugged. "Since I graduated from college. I guess I was about twenty-two."

"What was your relationship with Perry Dillon?"

Olympia went still. She shook her head, feigning confusion. "I'm sorry. *Who?*"

"He was an executive assistant for your uncle James." She made a disinterested face. "If you say so."

Liz accepted that and turned the page. Her eyes were riveted on the print in front of her. "What was your relationship with Sam Calvert?"

Everyone in the room tensed.

Olympia's expression went bland. "He was a field geologist. I received reports from him."

Liz made a note on the page in front of her. "On or off site?"

Olympia sat back in her chair, beginning to look resentful. "Both."

"And Allen Mullen?"

"He was an accountant."

"He conducted audits for Herndon Oil," Liz confirmed.

"Yes."

"And for a while he reported directly to you?"

Again Olympia hesitated. "Yes."

Liz turned another page, her expression matter-of-fact. "And all three of these gentlemen quit the company, did they not?"

Olympia fixed Liz with a killer glare. "If you say so."

"With rather large severance packages." Liz looked up, steady as a rock. "Is that correct?"

Olympia examined her manicure and toyed with the diamond on her right hand. "You'd have to talk to human resources...."

"Or perhaps just Perry Dillon, Sam Calvert and Allen Mullen," Liz suggested.

At that, Olympia paled.

Brockman Sr. leaned forward in his chair. "I don't know what's going on here."

But *his* lawyer did, Travis noted proudly.

Liz narrowed her eyes. "It would seem that what all three of these gentlemen have in common is that they all had sexual relations with Ms. Herndon. And when all three of their relationships with Ms. Herndon ended, abruptly and at her request, they found their careers in jeopardy. But not before each and every one of them did something to help Ms. Herndon advance her own agenda."

Olympia leaned forward, knowing, as did everyone in the room, that she had already lost. "You can't prove anything," she fumed.

Triumphant, Liz turned yet another page in her notebook. "Unfortunately for you, Ms. Herndon," she said in the deathly quiet that filled the room, "I can and have."

"How DID YOU KNOW where to look?" Travis asked Liz, when they got back to the hotel. No doubt about it, she had done a stellar job, better than he ever could have imagined, in bringing the campaign against him to a screeching halt.

Liz slipped off her heels and walked in her stockinged feet to the minibar. She opened it and pulled out two bottles of Texas-brewed beer. "The goats, believe it or not."

Travis thought about that as he twisted the top off the bottles and handed one back to her. "Queenie. Her sense of entitlement."

Liz found a glass and poured the golden liquid into it, being careful not to stir up too much foam. "The breeders said she apparently didn't know any other way to behave, no matter what situation they put her in." Liz set the half-empty bottle down and took a sip from her glass. "That led me to think about the fact that Olympia was an heiress."

Travis opened up the small fridge and rummaged around, bringing out a packet of mixed nuts and a bag of corn chips. He dropped them on the bed, took off his jacket and loosened his tie. "She certainly had a sense of entitlement."

"And power, both within the family company and her personal life." Liz sat down on the mattress. She set her glass on the nightstand and opened the chips. "Olympia used both to get what she wanted. I knew, given her age and the smooth but calculated way she operated, that it couldn't have been the first time she used a man to get what she wanted." Liz munched on a few chips and offered him some.

Their fingertips brushed as he accepted.

She let out a little sigh—the kind that made him want to haul her into his arms and kiss her—and continued her recitation. "So I knew, if Olympia wasn't exploiting her other attorneys, then she was definitely employing that same methodology somewhere else. Within her family company, where she quickly rose to power, was the logical place to look."

"Which is when you went to my grandfather, Hargett," Travis guessed, sitting down beside her.

Liz flushed.

Guilty as charged, he thought.

She reached for her glass, took another sip. "I know I should have talked to you about that first…"

Travis paused, bottle halfway to his lips. He set it back down on his thigh. "Why didn't you?" Hurt warred with the resentment within him.

Liz boldly met his gaze. "Because you would have argued with me and insisted it wasn't necessary—and we were running out of time."

Travis thought of how long they'd spent apart. Unnecessarily, in his view. "We could have asked for an extension," he pointed out casually.

"And we would have if we hadn't quickly found what we needed." Liz drained her glass and got up to retrieve the bottle.

Travis watched her pour the other half of her beer. "How did you find her other prey so quickly?" he asked when she returned to his side.

Liz sat down, facing him. "Hargett had the connections within the industry to ferret out any gossip, and the financial resources and private investigators on retainer to help locate the three gentlemen."

Travis covered her free hand with his own. "You talked to all three of them?"

"Yes." She exhaled and looked down.

He tightened his grip and felt her fingers curl into his. "And they were all willing to go on the record?"

Liz nodded and solemnly met his gaze. "They've had time to think about what happened. To regret selling out and moving on," she told him quietly.

Travis thought about how much he owed Liz. And the fact that his gratitude was only partially about the case. It went so much deeper.

He tilted the bottle to his lips and swallowed. "You think they'll sue her?"

Liz relaxed. "They can't. They waived that right when they accepted their generous severance packages. So there's no going back for them." She withdrew her hand and reached for the nuts.

"You, on the other hand, still have many avenues open to you." She balanced her glass on her thigh and opened the bag. "And the Herndons know it."

Travis studied her. "You really think Olympia will call it quits?"

Liz shook some nuts into his open palm. "It's either that or let the whole of Houston know she's been trading sexual favors for the benefit of her business dealings." Liz wrinkled her nose in distaste. "And since that's akin to personally prostituting herself—"

Her BlackBerry rang before she could finish. Liz went to get it. "Let's hope this is it!"

Amen to that. Although if it was, it would mean the end of this part of their relationship, Travis thought.

"Liz Cartwright. Yes." She closed her eyes and listened intently.

Travis's pulse picked up.

"I'll run it by my client and let you know."

She clicked off.

Travis leaned toward her. "What did they offer?"

Liz put the device down and did a happy dance. "First, all litigation against you has been withdrawn."

He lifted his hand and gave her a high five.

She sashayed closer and smacked her palm against his again. "As have the ethics and malpractice charges with the state bar of Texas."

Travis grinned. "That's great."

Liz twirled around, grabbed his hand and hauled him to his feet. "HB&R has offered their sincerest apologies for any misunderstanding that may have occurred. And they are offering you your old job back, with an immediate salary increase of fifteen percent."

Travis slung an arm around her waist and pulled her close.

"Should you choose not to take it—" still holding his hand, Liz spun away from him again "—they are prepared to offer you a very generous settlement, in exchange for you dropping your unlawful-termination lawsuit." She finished her announcement with a playful curtsy.

He gave Liz her due and bowed in respect.

When he rose again, he was grinning from ear to ear. As was she. Their glances met, held. Something joyous simmered between them. "We got everything we wanted," he told her softly.

Liz closed the distance between them and draped her arms about his neck. "You got your life back."

"I will," Travis promised gruffly. "Just as soon as I do this."

He lowered his head, and all the stress of the day— of the last few weeks—faded away. He was free again, free to pursue Liz the way he had wanted to ever since they'd met up again. Free to make her his in every way that counted. And as he dropped his head and kissed her, he knew what it felt like to belong with someone. Heart and soul.

And she longed for him, too. He felt it in the heat of her skin and the twining of their tongues, and the arch of her back as she pressed against him. The way she shifted close, went up on tiptoe and wreathed her arms about his neck told him she wanted and needed exactly what he did. A night filled with nothing but the two of them. A night based on passion and desire. Seduction and need... Intimacy and warmth.

Emotion spread through him. The only sounds in the room were their heavy breathing and her sudden gasp of pleasure as he opened her suit jacket and touched her breasts.

She moaned softly, her nipples pebbling against his palm. "I can't wait."

He nibbled her ear, then pulled back to look into her eyes. "You're going to have to, at least until we can get our clothes off...."

She seduced him with her laugh. Flushing, she pushed him away and reached back to undo the zipper on her skirt. It fell to floor, revealing beautiful hips and long sexy legs, and a thong that invited further inspection. His heart thudding, his body hard with anticipation, he murmured, "Allow me."

She smiled again, surrendering to him completely as he dropped to his knees and peeled off the panty hose, then the tiny scrap of lace.

"You're driving me crazy," she whispered in a hot, hungry voice.

"Exactly the point." He pressed his mouth between her breasts and kissed his way over warm flesh to the lace-covered nipples that had already tightened in arousal. She whimpered and caught his head between her hands. When he stroked his thumb through the auburn curls at her core, she trembled again and let out a cry that went straight through him.

"Then here's the next point." She gasped and moved away. "I want you naked, too. So..." she smiled at him wickedly "...allow me."

He shook his head. "Ladies first."

Still holding his gaze, she shrugged off her jacket. Let it fall.

"Only one piece left." He rose ever so slowly and stood before her once again.

Her emerald eyes darkened as he reached behind her and unclasped her bra. Drew it slowly off.

Quivering, she stood before him.

Damn, but she was beautiful. So beautiful he knew he would never tire of looking at her, being with her, making love with her.

Her eyes luminous, she murmured, "My turn."

He kissed her again, because he couldn't seem to stop, and she kissed him back just as avidly. Travis loved her like this, reckless and a little smug, determined to have what she wanted, when she wanted it, how she wanted it.

His hands went to her hair, loosening the complicated twist at the nape of her neck.

Her hands went to the buttons on his shirt. She undid them one by one, taking her time. Caressing his abs as she went.

Her hair fell to her shoulders. Slowly, his shirt came off and fluttered to the floor, next to her skirt.

She smiled again as she reached for his belt, then his zipper. She spread open his fly, slid her hands inside and wrapped her fingers around him, her palm closing knowingly over his erection.

He found her, too, and when she came apart for him, murmuring his name, his already racing pulse kicked into high gear. Catching her by the hips, he lifted her onto the bureau. Shifted her toward the edge. He kissed her again, his fingers caressing her gently before sliding into wet, hot silk.

"Now," she said, clutching at him. "I want you now, Travis."

He parted her thighs and stepped in close. She took all he had to give, rocking toward him, and he slid home. She wrapped her legs around his waist, encouraging him to go even deeper, to claim her as his for all time, and she exploded in pleasure.

TEN HOURS, TWO CALLS to room service and five bouts of lovemaking later, Liz and Travis were finally spent. "I wish we could stay like this forever," she murmured wistfully as they lay together, still wrapped in each other's arms.

Travis stroked a hand through her hair, pressed a

kiss on her temple. In a low, confused voice, he asked, "Why can't we?"

The practical side of her knew the heartbreaking truth. A shuddery sigh escaped her, but she refused to cry. There was too much emotion on her part already. Too much involvement for what had always been just a fling.

Liz swallowed, pulled herself together and sat up.

Needing cover, she slipped from the bed and went to find the white hotel robe. "We've got responsibilities," she said as she knotted the belt about her waist. She looked at the hotel coffeemaker and decided against starting it. Instead, she leaned against the bureau, bare legs crossed at the ankle, hands braced on either side of her.

Feigning an inner cheer she couldn't begin to feel, she said, "You have to decide what you're going to do with your life. I've got to go back to the ranch."

Travis shoved back the sheets and strode toward her in all his naked glory, flashing his bad-boy grin. He laughed at the look on her face, then dipped his head so that his mouth brushed her ear. "I know what I want to do with my life."

Realizing he wasn't as spent as she'd thought, she edged away. "Are you going to go back to HB&R?"

"Nope." His eyes were lit with heat, pleasure, and something even better—pride. "I'm taking their severance package and glowing recommendation."

Time seemed to stand still as their gazes collided. "And looking for a job with another big city firm."

Slowly, purposefully, he invaded her personal space. "No to that, too."

Liz slid a hand over his shoulder, ostensibly to hold him at bay. Although it felt more as if she was keeping him close. "Working for your grandfather, then?" Something else that would take him from Laramie County... and utilize his talents in a way he deserved?

Travis shook his head and leaned in, palms flat on the bureau on either side of her, trapping her in place. Then he kissed her, his tongue tantalizing hers softly, until she moaned.

She leaned back, knowing it was time—past time—that they were straight with each other. And themselves. "What then?"

His eyes grew shuttered. "I'm going back to the Four Winds."

Liz struggled against a myriad of emotions, none of which she really wanted to analyze. "For a few days."

He ran his thumb over her jaw. "For as long as you-all will have me."

With a gasp, she pushed free, then she stalked away, knowing she needed room to think.

Swallowing hard, she swung around once again. "You can't be serious."

He watched her tighten the belt on her robe. The heat of his gaze reminded her she was naked beneath.

"Why wouldn't I want to go back?" Travis countered in a low, husky voice. He waggled an eyebrow playfully, suggestively. "I've been happy there."

Heaven help her...so had she. "For a few weeks," she pointed out.

Travis shrugged his shoulders complacently. "I could be happy there the rest of my life."

If only, Liz thought with a disgruntled sigh. Unfortunately, she knew better. "I don't think so."

He blinked and stared at her, as if she were a stranger.

"We won, Travis. You got your life back." She drew

a deep breath and forced herself to be as strong as they both needed her to be. "You can go back to the life you built for yourself and the career you love."

He studied her, his expression inscrutable. "And leave you behind."

Surveying him just as cautiously, she shook her head. "That's not what I'm saying."

He tensed. "Then what *are* you saying?"

Liz shoved her hands through her hair and spun away from him again. "That we've been through a crisis together. A lot of emotions were involved."

He clamped a hand on her shoulder and turned her back to face him. "You bet they were involved," he exclaimed with exaggerated patience.

"It would be easy to mistake the closeness we felt while we worked toward a common goal as something else."

"Are we talking about you and me now?" His hold on her tightened possessively, then he dropped his hand. Stepped back. A muscle worked in his jaw. "Or you and your ex?"

Liz grasped the edge of the bureau to steady herself. "I've been down this road before. I know it feels like nothing has changed, but that's because we're still on a high after our victory. As days pass, things will calm down. What seems exciting and thrilling now may not feel quite so right then."

Travis folded his arms across his bare chest, not trying to conceal his irritation. "You're breaking up with me? And firing me, all in one fell swoop?"

Liz went on as if he hadn't spoken. "I'd like you to do as your family wants and take some time to really consider your options." Tears burned behind her eyes.

"I want you to figure out how you're going to pick up your career where you left off."

"I told you." His voice was as raw as the tension between them. "I don't want that."

"And I'm telling you if you walk away now, with some misguided notion of wanting to be with me, instead of pursuing what you've always wanted in a career, you will regret it. And when you do, you'll also blame me."

"So you're doing the noble thing and pushing me away first."

Giving him the space he needed was the best thing she could do for him. She cared enough about him— heck, she loved him enough—to make the sacrifice. "It's not like that."

"You're correct, Counselor. It isn't all about me and what I should have or what I want." He sounded as devastated as she felt. "This is about you, too, and your inability to make a real heart-and-soul commitment."

Liz clasped her hand to her chest. "That's not true."

"Right." Travis found his boxers and tugged them on. Then his pants. "You've got your law practice. You seem pretty devoted to that." He glared at her. "But as for anything else, like the ranch—or us—you can't seem to make a decision. One day you're in. The next day you're looking for a way out."

He snatched his shirt up off the floor and shrugged that on, too, then grabbed his tie. "You do just enough to avoid real conflict, and keep all your options open. Well, I'm not one of the fence sitters, Liz."

Travis sat down to put on his socks and shoes. "I don't want to think about it. I want a relationship with you."

When he was done, he stood up, towering over her

once again. "I want us to be together and maybe even have those babies your mother keeps hoping for." He touched her face as if for the very last time. "But it's not what you want."

He was right about that, Liz thought, bitterness welling up inside her.

She wanted a love that would last. Not the kind that felt good in the moment, under a special set of circumstances. Not a love that was destined to fade away. "So either I say yes to all that...?"

Travis dropped his hand and backed away. "Or it's over," he said very softly. "Plain and simple. You and I are history."

Liz caught her breath. She marched over and swung open the door. "Then you've got it," she told him furiously. "You and I are done."

Chapter Fifteen

Liz checked out of the hotel and returned to Laramie County the same way she had left it—alone. Reminding herself that this was what she had expected to happen all along, she stopped at her office and checked her messages. It seemed much had happened in her absence. Several new clients had called for appointments. Her mother had left a message, asking for a review of a contract at her earliest possible convenience. And the town's most irascible widower had phoned her, too.

"You're sure this is what you want to do?" Liz asked J.T. when she went over to his house a short while later to settle up with him and give him a ride.

J.T. carried his suitcase to the curb. In a boldly printed tropical shirt and shorts, walking shoes and a straw hat, he looked ready for the vacation he was about to embark upon.

He put his suitcase in the back, then climbed into the passenger seat and handed her a check for services rendered. "I think it's time I visited Hawaii. Don't you?"

Liz slid behind the wheel. "It probably makes more sense than putting in a lagoon-style swimming pool that may or may not get a lot of use." She started the engine. "How long are you planning to stay?"

J.T. shrugged affably. "I'm not sure. I rented a house

on the Big Island for the next six months. If I like it, I'll probably put my home here up for sale, and move there permanently."

Liz drove down Main Street and parked in front of the bus stop, next to the community center. "It's a big change."

"Your mother helped me realize that if I was ever going to recover from my loss, I'd have to get out of my rut and reinvent my life. It doesn't mean I love my late wife any less. I can honor her every day for the rest of my life, in my heart. It just means it's time to push on."

For all of us, Liz thought.

She offered J.T. her hand. "I hope it works out for you." She had a feeling it would. The widower seemed ready now to face the emotions he'd kept pent up inside. She wondered when she would be.

He clasped her palm warmly. "Thanks for all your help."

The bus that would take him to the Dallas/Fort Worth International Airport rumbled down the street.

Liz and J.T. said goodbye. She waved as he boarded, then headed back to her car.

By the time she reached her office, her mother was waiting for her, contracts in hand.

Reba took one look at her and held out her arms. "Oh, honey," she said.

Liz accepted her mother's hug, sinking into the warm maternal embrace.

"You won his case for him. And now he's not coming back."

Tears leaked from the corners of her eyes, adding to the pain in her heart. Damning her weakness where Travis was concerned, Liz choked out, "We knew it was only temporary." *That a relationship between us was never the goal.*

"Yet you hoped…" Reba said sympathetically.

Liz inhaled a jerky breath. Doing her best to pull herself together—she was a Cartwright woman, after all, and they were used to ill-fated romances—she straightened and blotted the moisture from her eyes. "Foolishly." Even though everything she had said and done had been to the contrary.

Reba took Liz's hand and guided her onto the waiting room sofa, then sat down beside her. "Just as I hoped you would one day take the reins managing the Four Winds."

Liz gulped, feeling a lump in her throat. It was past time for a heart-to-heart. "About that…"

Her mom held up a hand. "All your grandmothers or I have ever wanted is for you to be a cowgirl, just like us. For the longest time, we thought that meant doing what we had and taking over the running of the ranch." Reba paused. "But J.T. helped us see that we were in just as much of a rut as he was, and that we needed to reconfigure our way of thinking about the future, too."

"And what did you-all decide?"

"That the legendary Dale Evans was right. 'Cowgirl' is an attitude. It's about growing up proud and strong and having the courage to go after what you want, despite expectations to the contrary. A cowgirl faces life bravely. She follows her own heart and lives by her own rules."

Liz had done that, professionally. Her love life was another matter.…

"My heart is in my law practice," she told her mother sincerely. "But my home is on the Four Winds."

Reba searched her face. "Are you sure about that?"

Liz nodded with conviction. "I've lived in the city, Mom, remember? All that traffic, the people, the noise…it just wasn't for me. And there is no way I am moving back to town to be close to my office, so don't even suggest it. The ranch is my home. You are my family. The Four Winds is where I want to be."

"And where you'd like Travis to be, too."

Misery engulfed her. "I can't ask him to give up everything he fought so hard to get back."

Reba met her gaze. "So you're going to do what you did before. And just let him walk away, without a fight."

Liz lifted her chin proudly. "I can't make him want to stay." If he had, he would have already done so. No matter what she'd said or done.

I can't make him fall in love with me, the way I've already fallen in love with him.

Reba shook her head. "So instead you're pushing him away."

The ache in Liz's throat worsened. She had taken his case—and made love with him—to prove that she had gotten past the crushing hurt of their breakup. To demonstrate that she had moved on to a happy, defiantly single and bulletproof way of life. Only to discover she was even more vulnerable, and more in love with him, than ever.

Whereas Travis… He was still focused on his goals, and a future without her.

Liz swallowed. "It's the right thing, for both of us."

"Life has plenty of heartache without making more, out of fear and stubbornness. Cowgirl up, honey. If you want that man, go after him."

IT WAS FUNNY, Travis thought, as he walked into his grandfather's office on Monday afternoon, carrying a box of Hargett's favorite cigars and a bottle of whiskey. He'd thought redemption would feel a whole helluva lot better.

Instead, all he could think about was what he'd had—and lost. It had seemed as if he and Liz were getting a second chance. That his priorities, and her willingness to open herself up and let go, were finally in place. He'd thought they were going to do it right this time.

And they had.

It just hadn't lasted.

Hargett stood up from behind his desk and extended his hand with the vigor and strength of a much younger man. Behind him was the breathtaking view of downtown Houston.

"Liz phoned me earlier. I take it congratulations are in order?" Hargett asked, no small amount of pride in his voice as they greeted each other with a clap on the back and a firm handshake.

With gratitude welling up inside him for what his grandfather had done, Travis gave his palm an affectionate squeeze. "As well as a big thank-you."

"Don't thank me. Thank Liz." Hargett gestured for him to sit down. "In the beginning, I have to admit, I didn't understand why you hired that young woman to represent you." The oil man moved around his desk. "Now I know." He paused, looking Travis in the eye. "She's one hell of a good lawyer. Smart. Savvy. And determined to protect you and your interests."

"Which she did." Travis explained in detail what had happened at the deposition, as well as the settlement that had been reached.

Hargett nodded in approval. "Where is she now?"

Travis ignored the stab in his heart. "Back in Laramie County, I think."

His grandfather stared at him in amazement. "You don't know?"

"She left Houston yesterday." In fact, couldn't wait to get away.

Hargett settled in his chair thoughtfully. "Left the city or left you?"

Travis frowned, still hating it when the imperfections of his life were revealed. "What makes you think—?"

"C'mon, son, I know a woman whose heart is taken, even when she tries to hide it from me, like Liz did."

Travis set his jaw, stared out the window at the skyscraper across the street. Sunlight glinted off the black glass, as sharp and potent as the hurt inside him.

He exhaled and met his grandfather's probing gaze. "I think she cared about me, the way you care about a friend…." *I think she desired me, the way you desire someone you want to take to bed….*

Hargett scoffed. "Bull. The woman's in love with you."

Resentment tightened Travis's gut. *He wished.* "Not to hear her tell it."

The old man's eyebrows lifted in disbelief. "What's the problem? She doesn't want to leave Laramie County? 'Cause last time I checked there's plenty of space to land a helicopter on the Four Winds Ranch. And since the job of CEO of Anderson Oil comes with a chopper and pilot at your disposal…technically, you could live anywhere."

Travis grinned. The old guy could make quite a sales pitch when he wanted something. "Thanks for the offer," he replied genially.

Disappointment etched the craggy lines of his grandfather's face. "But you're not accepting," he guessed. "Even given the very nice formal offer I made."

Travis had to be honest. "Running a large corporation is not for me. It might be for one of my siblings, however."

Hargett sighed in regret. "I figured as much." He leaned back in his chair, rocking soundlessly, before straightening once again. "So what does this mean?" He propped his fingertips together. "You're going back to Haverty, Brockman & Roberts? Or on to greener pastures?"

Restless, Travis stood. "I'm not going backward. That never works." If it had, he and Liz would still be together. He wouldn't be standing here, feeling hurt and vulnerable as all get-out.

"But you are going back to the law?"

Travis strolled to the window and stood looking down at city streets that had lost their allure. "At least part-time."

"Planning to follow your parents' footsteps and start your own ranch, too?"

Travis shrugged and then slowly turned back around. More than anyone, his grandfather understood his need to be his own man. "I'd like to find a way to incorporate both in my life." Just as Liz had.

Hargett sent him a knowing look. "And you think working two jobs will make you happy."

Sliding his hands in his pockets, Travis inhaled deeply. "If my recent mistakes and the resulting crisis have taught me anything, it's that I want a more well-rounded life." A home and a woman to love, and love him back, and a family of his very own to come home to at night.

"Then," Hargett announced, smiling slowly, "there's only one way to get that."

LIZ SPENT THE NEXT FEW days getting caught up on work, meeting with clients and thinking about what to do regarding her love life. Or current lack thereof. And she was still thinking about the best way to remedy the mistakes she had made when she parked her car in the drive, grabbed her briefcase and walked into the Four Winds ranch house.

Her mother greeted her in the foyer. Faye Elizabeth and Tillie were right behind her. All beamed with an unusual degree of excitement.

"Put your boots on, honey!" Reba ordered cheerfully, engulfing her in a warm hug. "And ride out to see our new guard donkeys. They're in pasture 23 with the goats."

Liz barely had time to draw a breath, never mind formulate a response, as Tillie clapped her hands in excitement. "They really are a sight to behold."

Faye Elizabeth nodded, a twinkle in her eyes. "They're all just darling. You don't want to miss it."

Relieving Liz of her briefcase and purse, Reba directed, "And ride your horse! You look like you need some R & R. And so does your mare."

Liz could have refused, in favor of going after Travis first via heartfelt letter, then a phone call, and finally a weekend-long date. But she couldn't ignore the needs of her pet, after the days away. She winced guiltily, then said, "You're right. My horse does need the exercise." And the time outdoors would give her a chance to better formulate a plan.

Travis was big on well-executed plans.

"Tell you what," Reba offered, oblivious to Liz's real focus. "I'll saddle her up for you while you change clothes."

Liz pushed the image of Travis—so handsome, and hurting—away.

"I'll pack you a picnic," Tillie offered.

Travis would forgive her.

Liz hadn't lost her chance.

Not this time.

Not if she had anything to say about it.

"As long as you're taking a break, it never hurts to have a little music, and a blanket for chilling out," Faye Elizabeth declared with enthusiasm.

Liz lifted her hand, with a grin. "Hold the wagon, ladies! I'm going, I'm going!"

By the time she got back downstairs, in her favorite old jeans, flat-brimmed hat, boots and calico shirt, her gear was ready to go. "Aren't any of you coming with me?" she asked.

Tillie waved her away. "We have too much to do here."

Reba nodded. "You enjoy yourself, though."

Liz supposed she shouldn't be surprised by the all-out effort to get her to take some time to herself and cheer up. She'd been down in the dumps ever since she and Travis had split up.

Determined to use the time wisely—maybe even start mentally composing the love letter she intended to write to him—Liz headed out. Minutes later, she was riding down the path past the empty homestead.

Trying not to think about how lonely she felt, Liz kept going.

She had already tried a breezy, informal, let's-stay-friends approach to fixing things. Unfortunately, calling him hadn't netted any response. So she had tried texting and asking how everything was going, as a less pressured way of opening the door.

Only to receive the cryptic response: Getting better by the day—thanks to you. T.

It was the kind of semiformal response one sent a business acquaintance.

She knew that shouldn't surprise her. She had turned down his proposal that they keep seeing each other, and had pushed him toward a life that had no room for her in it. Then selfishly decided she wanted him back.

Meanwhile, he was completely focused on the future. His future.

Not theirs.

But he would have been, Liz realized, spurring her horse into a gallop, if she had only been brave enough to go after what she wanted.

All this time, she had focused on what was right for other people. For Travis, when he'd been fixated on all those lofty goals and leaving for college. For her family, when they were struggling to keep the ranch operating and bring her more fully back into the family business. For her clients, as she built her law practice.

Liz bent over the horse, feeling the wind in her face. She hadn't ever let herself think much about what was right for her. Hadn't let herself take the risk of going after the man she wanted with everything she had, for fear she would end up like all the other Cartwright women—alone, with a broken heart, a victim of fate and circumstance.

That had been her real mistake, Liz thought, as she rode over the ridge that bordered pasture 23. Refusing to risk her dignity for happiness.

She took a deep, rejuvenating breath and slowed the pace of her horse to a gentle trot. Gazing down below, she noted that there were two donkeys and twelve goats in the green pasture. All was peaceful.

Then the horse and cowboy standing next to the fence caught her eye. He had his back to her, but she knew the set of those strong shoulders, recognized those long muscular legs.

Heart pounding, she rode closer, wanting so much to take every hard inch of him into her arms.

She slid off her horse and walked toward him.

Her mare headed for his beloved quarter horse.

Travis turned and eyed her for a long moment, saying nothing, as together, their horses began to graze.

"What are you doing out here?" Liz asked inanely.

Was he an active part of the matchmaking going on at the Four Winds? Or just an unsuspecting victim of it, like her?

He indicated the pasture to their left and his mouth quirked slightly. "I've been doing a little research on donkeys."

Yet another surprise, given his disinterest in anything but cattle, dogs and horses on a ranch. Liz stepped closer and tilted her head, letting him take the lead. "Is that right?"

His eyes turned a warmer hue. "They live thirty to forty years, when cared for properly."

"I didn't know that," she murmured, while her heart continued to pound.

"They like working in pairs," he stated, catching her hand in his and drawing her close.

He looked down at her with so much tenderness she could barely breathe.

"Once they've bonded with a friend, separation is very stressful."

Liz nodded, shifting near enough to smell the leather-and-spice scent of his skin.

"And they also grow attached to people." Travis's hand slid down her spine, soothing, massaging, guiding her blissfully close. "They're gentle with children and calm around strangers, and they give as well as receive love."

He dipped his head and ran his lips across her temple.

She drew a shuddery breath and clutched at him.

"They like to nuzzle and cuddle," he continued, with a seriousness that made her worries start to fade away. "They're sweet, vigilant, powerfully spiritual creatures who protect their herd or family." Travis wrapped both arms around her waist and held her close, his strength as overpowering as his presence. "We have a lot to learn from them."

"Yes…" Liz's heart somersaulted in her chest. Knowing that whatever happened, she wasn't going to let him go without a fight, she met his eyes and whispered, "I guess we do."

His voice was low and husky, his gaze intent. "I wasn't honest with you. I'm sorry," he said in her ear, running his palm up and down her spine. "I should have told you what I wanted from you from the beginning."

Beneath his shirt, she could feel the steady beating of his heart. Lower still, the heat and strength of his desire. Liz hitched in a bolstering breath. "I should have been more forthright with you, too."

His eyes filled with warmth. "I want a helluva lot more than friendship and sex. I want your love, Liz. I want you to love me as much as I love you."

Tears of joy slipped down her face at the words she had so longed to hear. Liz stood on tiptoe and kissed him soundly. "Oh, Travis!" Her whole body trembled with the emotion she'd been holding back. "I do love you. So very, very much."

And to prove it, she kissed him, putting her whole heart and soul into the embrace. He kissed her back, again and again and again, until there was no more negotiating, no more disbelief. Only the reality that they were going to be together, from here on out.

"So what next?" she asked tremulously at last, knowing if they stayed here and kept kissing, they wouldn't be clothed for very long. "Where do we go from here?"

Travis grinned and waggled his eyebrows. "To bed?"

She laughed. "Definitely to bed." She kissed him again, letting him know how aroused she was. "And after…?"

Drawing back slightly, he sobered, caressing her face with the flat of his palm. "I thank you for making it possible," he told her quietly, "but I'm not going back to my old way of life. No more big-city law firms. No more single-minded, goal-driven agendas. From now on, I'm going to be taking a much more balanced approach." He kissed her slowly, sweetly. "I'm going to be focusing on ranching and being with family—yours and mine—and paving my own future as a solo gas and oil attorney. But most of all, I'm going to be pursuing and wooing you."

She felt her heart catch at the way he looked at her. "You already have me," she told him, joy spiraling through her.

He let out a very masculine sigh of satisfaction. Entwining their fingers, he brought her hand up to his mouth and brushed his lips across it. "I want more than what we've had so far. I want us to be together for the rest of our lives."

"I think we can manage that." She could see them getting married one day. Running a ranch together. Having a family...

"And let's promise not to walk away at the first sight of trouble," Travis proposed, looking deep into her eyes. "We're going to get it right this time."

Liz stood on tiptoe and kissed him with all the love she had in her heart. Forever sounded very good indeed. "You bet we will."

Epilogue

One year later...

"It's about time the two of you expanded," Tillie told Travis and Liz.

Liz viewed the four generations sitting around the kitchen table at the Four Winds. Much had changed in the year since she and Travis had officially become a couple.

Travis had used some of his severance money from his old employer and bought into the ranch. The infusion of cash had paid for fancy new equipment, which made the land management a heck of a lot easier. The herd of goats and donkeys had been expanded, as had their cattle operation. An additional barn was built, a full-time cowboy hired.

Reba surveyed the blueprints spread over the kitchen table. "Updating and adding on to the homestead won't be as cost-effective as starting from scratch."

"True," Travis said, viewing the planned two-story, three-thousand-square-feet abode. "But it will be worth it in sentimental value."

"The Four Winds Ranch started with that cabin," Faye Elizabeth murmured nostalgically, as she looked over the plans, which contained two home offices, three bedrooms, and two and a half baths. "Every Cartwright bride has stayed there the very first year of her marriage."

Liz beamed, thinking of all the wonderfully romantic times she and Travis had shared in the rustic cozy abode. Only now, instead of just a bed and a bath and a hot plate, they'd have a full-size kitchen and laundry room, too. "Including me."

"Three babies have been conceived in that cabin," Tillie reminisced fondly.

"Hey. I thought lobbying for grandchildren was my job," Reba teased. "Especially now that they've been married for almost six months…"

Liz blushed, as she thought about all the intimate talks and passionate lovemaking and cuddling that had gone on there. No doubt about it, she and Travis were closer than she'd ever thought a man and a woman could be. And with every day that passed, they seemed more connected and in tune with each other.

Reading her mind, Travis wrapped his arm about her waist and tucked her to his side. "Shall we tell them all our news?" he asked quietly.

She nodded, deciding to start with work. "Travis and I are taking our solo law firms and combining them."

"Liz's name will go first, since she's been established longer, and mine second."

"So it will be Cartwright Anderson, LLP. Travis will head up the oil and gas attorneys—we're planning to hire a few associates to work with us—and I'll head up mediation and litigation services."

Tillie, Reba and Faye Elizabeth all murmured their excited approval.

"We're also going to hire—if it's okay with you ladies—a nighttime hired hand, to go along with the Four

Winds weekday cowboy." She and Travis still helped out on nights and weekends, but that was going to have to be curtailed as their other duties expanded.

"Any particular reason why?" Tillie asked slyly.

Liz took her husband's wrist and kissed the back of it. "Do you want to tell them or shall I?"

Travis chuckled and slipped a possessive hand to her belly. "Let's let them guess."

Reba clapped a hand to her chest, looking so deliriously happy she might faint. "You're pregnant?" she cried with delight.

Liz and Travis nodded. "The due date is January 12," Liz revealed in a voice hoarse with emotion.

A boisterous cheer went up.

"Hallelujah!" the women chorused. Liz and Travis were jubilantly embraced by all. "We hoped the day would come when you both would get everything you ever wanted!"

And they had, Liz thought happily. For now…and forever.

* * * * *

HEART & HOME

Harlequin®

American Romance®

COMING NEXT MONTH
AVAILABLE APRIL 10, 2012

#1397 BABY'S FIRST HOMECOMING
Mustang Valley
Cathy McDavid

A year after Sierra Powell gave her baby up for adoption, little Jamie was returned to her. Determined to make a new life for both of them, she returns to Mustang Valley to reunite with her estranged family. But she doesn't expect to run into Clay Duvall, a former enemy of the Powells...and the secret father of her son.

#1398 THE MARSHAL'S PRIZE
Undercover Heroes
Rebecca Winters

#1399 TAMED BY A TEXAN
Hill Country Heroes
Tanya Michaels

#1400 THE BABY DILEMMA
Safe Harbor Medical
Jacqueline Diamond

You can find more information on upcoming Harlequin® titles, free excerpts and more at www.Harlequin.com.

HARCNM0312

REQUEST YOUR FREE BOOKS!
2 FREE NOVELS PLUS 2 FREE GIFTS!

§Harlequin®

American ☆ Romance®

LOVE, HOME & HAPPINESS

YES! Please send me 2 FREE Harlequin® American Romance® novels and my 2 FREE gifts (gifts are worth about $10). After receiving them, if I don't wish to receive any more books, I can return the shipping statement marked "cancel." If I don't cancel, I will receive 4 brand-new novels every month and be billed just $4.49 per book in the U.S. or $5.24 per book in Canada. That's a saving of at least 14% off the cover price! It's quite a bargain! Shipping and handling is just 50¢ per book in the U.S. and 75¢ per book in Canada.* I understand that accepting the 2 free books and gifts places me under no obligation to buy anything. I can always return a shipment and cancel at any time. Even if I never buy another book, the two free books and gifts are mine to keep forever.

154/354 HDN FEP2

Name _____ (PLEASE PRINT) _____

Address _____ Apt. # _____

City _____ State/Prov. _____ Zip/Postal Code _____

Signature (if under 18, a parent or guardian must sign) _____

Mail to the Reader Service:
IN U.S.A.: P.O. Box 1867, Buffalo, NY 14240-1867
IN CANADA: P.O. Box 609, Fort Erie, Ontario L2A 5X3

Not valid for current subscribers to Harlequin American Romance books.

Want to try two free books from another line?
Call 1-800-873-8635 or visit www.ReaderService.com.

* Terms and prices subject to change without notice. Prices do not include applicable taxes. Sales tax applicable in N.Y. Canadian residents will be charged applicable taxes. Offer not valid in Quebec. This offer is limited to one order per household. All orders subject to credit approval. Credit or debit balances in a customer's account(s) may be offset by any other outstanding balance owed by or to the customer. Please allow 4 to 6 weeks for delivery. Offer available while quantities last.

Your Privacy—The Reader Service is committed to protecting your privacy. Our Privacy Policy is available online at www.ReaderService.com or upon request from the Reader Service.

We make a portion of our mailing list available to reputable third parties that offer products we believe may interest you. If you prefer that we not exchange your name with third parties, or if you wish to clarify or modify your communication preferences, please visit us at www.ReaderService.com/consumerschoice or write to us at Reader Service Preference Service, P.O. Box 9062, Buffalo, NY 14269. Include your complete name and address.

HARI1B

◆ Harlequin® *Romance*

*Get swept away with a brand-new miniseries
by* **USA TODAY** *bestselling author*

MARGARET WAY

The Langdon Dynasty

Amelia Norton knows that in order to embrace her future,
she must first face her past. As she unravels her family's secrets,
she is forced to turn to gorgeous cattleman Dev Langdon for
support—the man she vowed never to fall for again.

Against the haze of the sweltering Australian heat Mel's
guarded exterior begins to crumble...and Dev will do
whatever it takes to convince his childhood sweetheart
to be his bride.

THE CATTLE KING'S BRIDE

Available April 2012

And look for
ARGENTINIAN IN THE OUTBACK

Coming in May 2012

www.Harlequin.com

HR17799

Taft Bowman knew he'd ruined any chance he'd had for happiness with Laura Pendleton when he drove her away years ago...and into the arms of another man, thousands of miles away. Now she was back, a widow with two small children...and despite himself, he was starting to believe in second chances.

Harlequin Special® Edition® presents a new installment in USA TODAY *bestselling author RaeAnne Thayne's miniseries,* THE COWBOYS OF COLD CREEK.

Enjoy a sneak peek of
A COLD CREEK REUNION

Available April 2012 from Harlequin® Special Edition®

A younger woman stood there, and from this distance he had only a strange impression, as though she was somehow standing on an island of calm amid the chaos of the scene, the flashing lights of the emergency vehicles, shouts between his crew members, the excited buzz of the crowd.

And then the woman turned and he just about tripped over a snaking fire hose somebody shouldn't have left there.

Laura.

He froze, and for the first time in fifteen years as a firefighter, he forgot about the incident, his mission, just what the hell he was doing here.

Laura.

Ten years. He hadn't seen her in all that time, since the week before their wedding when she had given him back his ring and left town. Not just town. She had left the whole damn country, as if she couldn't run far enough to get away from him.

Some part of him desperately wanted to think he had made some kind of mistake. It couldn't be her. That was just some other slender woman with a long sweep of honey-blond hair and big, blue, unforgettable eyes. But no. It was definitely Laura. Sweet and lovely.

Not his.

He was going to have to go over there and talk to her. He didn't want to. He wanted to stand there and pretend he hadn't seen her. But he was the fire chief. He couldn't hide out just because he had a painful history with the daughter of the property owner.

Sometimes he hated his job.

Will Taft and Laura be able to make the years recede...or is the gulf between them too broad to ever cross?

Find out in
A COLD CREEK REUNION
Available April 2012 from Harlequin® Special Edition®
wherever books are sold.

Celebrate the 30th anniversary
of Harlequin® Special Edition® with a bonus story
included in each Special Edition® book in April!

Copyright © 2012 by RaeAnne Thayne

HSEEXP0412